PORTRAITS IN DIGNITY

Eva Bell

INDIA • SINGAPORE • MALAYSIA

ISBN 979-8-88815-644-5

Dedication

For Vivienne Deepa

who believes that women as persons of dignity and worth

must fight against gender-based abuse.

CONTENTS

ACKNOWLEDGEMENTS

Romona and Manfred Anton for their support.

Suman Sapre for proof reading.

Franklin Bell for valuable inputs.

AUTHOR'S NOTE

The charm of a woman's personality is the manner in which she conveys her self-confidence and redefines her feminity by taking life into her own hands, making her own choices and conveying to the world that dignity is non-negotiable.

PORTRAITS IN DIGNITY is a collection of twelve short stories that highlight the many evils that young Indian women are subjected to and their brave efforts to liberate themselves from the boundaries that restrict their blossoming into womanhood. Parts of the country are still enslaved by casteism, gender issues, domestic violence, prostitution and sexual harassment. Trafficking in young girls is rampant in some parts of the country. The women in these stories recognise their capabilities and their limitations, and strive towards defining their individuality as daughters, mothers or wives. Each ends on a positive note and will be an inspiration to women in similar circumstances.

As Florence Kennedy counselled, "You've got to rattle your cage door. You've got to let them know that you're in there. Make noise, cause trouble. You may not win right away but you'll sure have a lot of fun."

PINK MAGNOLIA

Nimmo stretched and rolled on to her side, pulling the patchwork quilt over her head.

"Wake up Child," her mother called for the third time. "Your father has invited a friend. We must have a meal ready before he arrives."

"Just a little longer Mother. It's still dark outside and cold too."

Her mother's eyes rested on her brood of children – seven of them, and the youngest only three years old! They were stretched out on the floor in different stages of slumber.

"Like fish laid out for sale in the market place," she sighed, "and the eldest ready to go."

Her eyes lingered on Nimmo, her firstborn. She was like a pink magnolia bursting into bloom in spring.

"I will miss her. But with so many mouths to feed, we need money and she must go to the city to work. There's not much life left in her father. He keeps coughing at night and sometimes, he can hardly breathe. All those years of puffing on his *bidis* have taken their toll."

She called again. "Nimmo, that's enough of sleep. Wake up at once."

The girl arched her back like a lazy cat and stretched out her long limbs. A sudden growth spurt made her look tall for her age. Her body was filling out too, as she blossomed into adolescence. She rubbed her sleepy eyes and sat up, then folded her quilt and rolled up her rush mat. She stood it in the corner and went out to perform her morning ablutions before the routine chores of the day began.

She had just finished making the *rotis* when she heard voices in the courtyard. Her father's voice was raised in greeting.

"Welcome to our humble hut, Sahib," he said, as he spread out a mat for the guest.

Her mother left what she was doing and hurried out too.

Nimmo peeped through the solitary window. The three of them were talking in hushed tones. The man raised his head and she froze when she recognized him.

"This is the same man I saw at the water tap. He was trying to make conversation with all of us. I didn't like the way he looked us up and down and smiled, as though harbouring some secret."

Her mother called. "Nimmo, bring some tea for our guest."

She put two thick *rotis* on an aluminium plate with a spoonful of potato *sabzi* and a tall glass of milky tea. She didn't like the way his eyes followed her and travelled up and down her body. He grinned, revealing a bit of silver on his front tooth. She was both repulsed and frightened.

"How did my father make his acquaintance?" she wondered, "and why is he here so early in the day?"

She went indoors and refused to come out again. But when he was gone, she accosted her mother.

"Who is that man? He was at the water tap two days ago and was trying to act familiar with all of us."

"He's just trying to help. You know how poor we are. Your father is so weak, he can't work for long. This man has made some suggestions but you don't have to worry. Let's leave it to your father."

The village was in a lush valley near the Indo-Nepalese border. From her courtyard, on a clear day she could see the peaks of the Kanchenjunga. The family owned a few yaks and a small patch of land on which grew apples and peaches. But it barely supported them. Nimmo's father was a labourer in the orchards and farms of the rich. But come winter, life in the hills was at a standstill for three whole months. It was a hard life. Except for the two youngest children, everyone had to work. Sometimes, there wasn't enough food to go around and the children would grow fretful.

But Nimmo had a way about her. She knew how to make her siblings laugh when they wanted to cry. Sometimes, she took them along to the house of a reclusive writer, who had made his home in their village. She cooked and cleaned for him. He gave her a decent salary, and allowed her to take home surplus food which he couldn't finish. In his spare time, he taught Nimmo and the elder children how to read and write. Many evenings, after the lesson, he would tell them a story he had just written, carefully listening to their comments. Gregory Sahib was a writer of children's stories and they loved him. He brought sunshine into their lives.

The man with the silver tooth called at their hut three times. On each occasion Nimmo saw him whispering to her parents who nodded their agreement to whatever he said.

Her mother never confided in her anymore. After each visit, she grew more silent. Sometimes, Nimmo caught her wiping her eyes. On his last visit, money had changed hands. She saw her father eagerly grab the bundle from the man, who bellowed like the burp of a gluttonous hyena and thumped her father on his back.

"What is Father doing?" she wondered, "Is the man a money lender? Will we ever be able to pay him back?"

That evening, she trudged up the hill to Gregory Sahib's house by herself. She would have to tell him about this horrible man who had been dropping by so frequently. But there was a lock on the door. The watchman said that the writer had received good news about his book and had gone to Delhi to find out more.

That night, when the other children were asleep, Nimmo's parents called her outside.

"Nimmo, we have good news for you. The man, who has been visiting us, has found a job for you in the city. You are to work in the house of a rich lady who will not only look after you, but pay you a good salary. You can keep some pocket money for yourself and ask her to send the rest to us. If you don't like the job, you can come back after six months."

Nimmo burst into tears. "I don't trust that man, Mother. He has a wicked look in his eyes. I don't want to go… I'll miss my brothers and sisters."

"Enough of that," said her father gruffly, "you better pack your things quickly and I'll take you down to the bus stop. He will be waiting there. This wouldn't have happened if I had a grown-up son. But the Gods have cursed me – four daughters in a row, then a son who keeps falling ill all the time, and then two more girls. You're not good for farm work. You could do a better job cooking and cleaning for the lady."

"But I'm already working for Gregory Sahib and he pays well."

"The lady will pay enough to support the whole family. Now you behave well with the man. He is very kind."

Between sobs, Nimmo bundled the two threadbare saris and blouses she possessed. She reached up under the eaves and found her comb, a broken piece of mirror and a round tin with her trinkets. She slipped two red plastic bangles on her hands.

"I'm taking my quilt, Mother," she said, "At least I'll have something to hold on to when I'm homesick."

It was a multi-coloured patchwork quilt put together crudely with coarse stitches, and had taken almost a year to finish. She had collected scraps of cloth from the tailor's shop whenever she went to the marketplace.

"I wonder if I'll ever see you all again," she sobbed, bending down to kiss her sleeping siblings. Then she hugged her mother who quietly slipped a small pouch into her hands. It contained her last salary from Gregory Sahib.

Her father coughed and spluttered all the way down to the bus stop, but never said a word to her.

"It's all because of him," she thought angrily, "can't do a man's work and support his family."

She remembered the times when the Public Health nurse had visited their hut and advised him to stop smoking those infernal *bidis*. She even scolded him for having a hut full of children who were all weak and skinny.

"Do I have to leave home to pay for his stupidity?" she wondered. "If only I were a boy!"

To her surprise, three of her friends were also waiting at the bus stop. Their faces were swollen from crying. Each exclaimed on seeing her, "Has the man found a job for you too?"

"Yes, my parents say he's a kind man. He has seen how poor we are and has found a way to help our families."

Ram Ghising, for that was his name, walked jauntily down the road, his Nepalese cap tilted to a rakish angle on his head. His silver tooth shone under the rays of the street lamp.

"I'm glad you are all here. Now get into the bus, all of you. No giggling or jabbering. No crying either. You must get some sleep on the bus tonight. We'll reach the plains only at dawn. There we'll catch the Express train to Bombay."

Sleep was long in coming. It was 'goodbye' to the hills and to all the people Nimmo loved and cared about. If only she could have bid farewell to Gregory Sahib! He would think her ungrateful to have left without a word.

The girls, though worried over their future, took comfort from the fact that they had each other. They slept fitfully, waking up each time to make sure that they were all together.

By early morning, they had reached the plains. Being unaccustomed to the heat, they began to fidget and grumble. Ram Ghising herded them into the train and cautioned,

"Take care that you don't chat with people in your compartment. It will take a little over two days to reach our destination. Be on your best behaviour. I'll be watching."

He had booked berths for them in a three-tier compartment and arranged for meals to be served periodically on the train. However, he travelled in a different compartment and kept his distance. The girls noticed that at every major stop, he would walk past the compartment to check if they were all there.

"Are you all sisters?" asked a lady in the compartment, "Where are you going? Are you travelling by yourselves?"

The other three girls knew a smattering of Hindi, but as Gregory Sahib had been teaching Nimmo to read and write, she could speak well. But she remained silent.

"If that man comes to know I have talked to the lady, who knows what punishment he'll have in store for me!"

However, she listened intently to the conversation of the other passengers. The talk was mostly uninteresting. There was one couple however, who sat in a corner and kept staring at them.

"Hmm! Nepali girls!" she snorted, "We know where they are heading. Do you think they have run away from home? Going to the big, bad city to earn a living I presume. What kind of greedy, irresponsible parents they must have!"

Nimmo almost lashed out at the woman. Then she remembered she was not to utter a word. But the woman continued talking.

"Dear, do you think we should inform the police when we get off the train?"

Nimmo froze. "Good God! What is going to happen to us? Where is the evil man taking us?"

She pulled out the quilt from her bag and draped it around her shoulders. Suddenly she began to shiver, though everybody else was grumbling about the heat.

"Nimmo, why are you shivering? Are you feeling ill?" the other girls worried.

"No, just homesick. I'll be alright. Don't worry."

But she couldn't get over the uncomfortable feeling that something terrible was going to happen to them all.

When they alighted at Bombay very early on the third day, Nimmo looked around for the lady who threatened to call the police. But Ram Ghising whisked them off even before many passengers could reach for their luggage. They drove in a taxi for a very long time, until they left the city and reached a distant suburb.

"What a wonderful city!" one of the girls exclaimed, "and so many people!"

"The cars and buses are making my head spin," said another.

"And see those posters – Shah Rukh Khan and Rani – they showed that movie in our Cinema hall. They live in Bombay. I wonder if I'll get to see them drive past in their cars."

Only Nimmo remained silent. A deep sadness enveloped her.

"Will I ever go home again," she wondered. "Mother said I could return after six months if I didn't like the job. But will Ram Ghising ever let me?"

The taxi drew up before a tall apartment. It stood out against the grey distemper of the adjoining flats. The façade was in a light shade of maroon and the cream-coloured door looked inviting. The windows on the first and second floors had bright printed curtains which fluttered in the breeze. Red and yellow potted rose bushes bordered the few steps that led up to the door. Ram Ghising pressed the doorbell. Earlier, he had shaken Nimmo by her shoulder.

"You girl, I'll tolerate none of your sulks. Now if you know what's good for you, give the lady your best smile," he barked.

Though she remained mute, Ram drew back at the fury in her eyes.

"This one is not going to be easy," he thought, "but Madam will know how to bring her to her knees. That will serve her right. I can picture an unsuspecting client attacked by this tigress. Boy, if I wasn't in such a hurry to get rid of this lot, I'd have loved to wrestle with her myself."

The door opened and the girls were rushed indoors. Ram Ghising brought in the rear. His pseudo humility and sycophancy before the gorgeous lady in the armchair irritated Nimmo. The girls gaped at the lady.

"Is this our employer?" they wondered. "What work would she have for four maids?"

"Don't stand there staring," Ram scolded, "Fold your hands together and bow."

Madam Aum was a pretty lady. She also had a kind voice.

"Girls, go into the next room," she said, "you must be tired after your long journey. I'll be with you just as soon as I finish my business with Ram. Do you want to say 'goodbye' to him? It will be a while before you see him again."

The three girls sobbed as if they were taking leave of a beloved relative. But Nimmo turned away to hide the anger in her eyes. Madam Aum sensed trouble.

"I wonder if Ram has been acting fresh with her. Below this veneer of humility, I know he's not just a greedy sod but a lecher too. I must find out what's bugging her. I like my employees to be happy. It's the best way to keep my business running smoothly."

She turned to Ram who had a worried look on his face.

"If Madam doesn't like the girl, she'll ask me to take her back. That's impossible. I can't be seen in her village in the near future and I can't drag her along with me, hunting for a new Madam. It's too risky. I'm already on the Activists' black list. If I'm caught, it will be prison for me."

Nimmo stood close behind the door, her ears cocked to tune into their conversation. They had been served tea and biscuits until breakfast was ready, and the other girls were slurping the stuff from small stainless steel tumblers. Nimmo leaned against the door.

"Twenty thousand for each girl," she heard Madam say. "Half must go to their parents."

"Then what's in it for me Madam?" Ram whined, "It's a pittance for all the trouble I've taken and the money I've spent on them. I've already paid a tidy sum to each family."

"It's much more than I gave you last time, considering that all of them were disappointing. Two fell ill and had to be sent away. I wonder if they ever got cured and found their way home."

Nimmo gasped. No, she had to be very silent if she must hear the rest.

"And the other two were cunning devils who eloped with the customers," continued Madam.

"It's a risk I'm taking with this lot and I'm not willing to pay a rupee more. On the contrary,

I can see that one girl is not as docile as the rest. She is going to give me a lot of trouble."

Nimmo bent down and peeped through the key hole.

"Hey, what are you looking at? Give us a chance too," the others said.

"It's nothing. If you don't keep quiet, we'll all be punished by Madam."

But Nimmo had seen enough. Madam had pulled out a bulky pouch from her waist band and handed a bundle of crisp notes to Ram. He didn't look happy. The humble attitude he had first adopted seemed to have vanished. Nimmo realised that Madam had bought them for a price. They would have to obey her, though they didn't as yet know the nature of the work they were expected to do. Nimmo hoped that she was a good woman.

Madam Aum was pretty and fair of complexion with dark expressive eyes.

"So unlike ours," Nimmo thought.

Her hair was held back in a clasp, revealing star-shaped ear studs that sparkled like diamonds. She was well proportioned, neither too slim nor too fat, except for a tiny roll of flesh that peeped out between her blouse and waistline.

"You must all be very tired. Come, I'll take you to your rooms. You need to have a good bath and a hearty breakfast. After that, a few hours of sleep will do you a world of good."

She led the way to the third floor.

"There are people living on the first and second floors. So be as quiet as you can," she cautioned.

It was a large airy room with four beds. Each had a cupboard to store their things.

"I have left soap and a towel for each one of you. Make sure you give yourself a good scrub. Do you have clean clothes to wear? If not, there are saris in each of your cupboards.

When ready, come down to the dining room as softly as you can. As I said, there are others living in this apartment. They need their rest."

"We've never slept on anything but mats before. Do you think sleep will come?" one of them asked.

"Oh yes," said Nimmo, "I've seen such beds in Gregory Sahib's house. The mattress is soft and spongy. We'll be asleep even before our heads touch the pillows. Madam Aum seems to be a good lady. I think we'll be happy here. Now I'll go for my bath."

She took the cake of soap left for her use. It had a mild perfume which she liked. In her cupboard there were three saris. Perhaps Madam's cast-offs. But they were laundered and fresh. Nimmo decided she would wear her own clothing on the first day. Her sari had been washed in the clear spring water behind her house. It smelt of the hills and made her feel near to her family. But it brought on a bout of homesickness that made her eyes moist. She rushed off for a leisurely bath.

When they trooped into the dining hall for breakfast, Madam looked up from what she was doing. She quietly assessed each one. Many young women had passed through her hands, but none so young and pristine pure as these. For all practical purposes, she was licensed to run a working women's hostel. Though the authorities knew what kind of work they indulged in, they turned a blind eye as there had never been a law and order problem here. Besides, Madam kept the palms of the important officials well-greased. However, using underage girls was a crime which could bring severe penalties or even invite a jail sentence. Some of her customers wanted young virgins. They believed this had some therapeutic effect on several sexual maladies and were willing to pay well.

"They are like fresh mountain blossoms. Will they survive the heat and dust of the city?" she wondered. "What's more, can they deliver what my clients crave for? Can they survive the rough and tumble of this dirty business?"

Madam Aum had come to terms with her conscience years ago. Hers was a business like any other. Only her merchandise happened to be humans. They had feelings and emotions of love, hate, sadness and joy. As time went by, their anger and pain would give way to a frightening coldness. Gradually they would turn into mere automatons, performing for insatiable clients.

Of late, Madam had many sleepless nights, wondering what kind of hell was reserved for her when she died. Would it be eternal damnation? Would she be reincarnated into a pig or a dog?

"Why have I suddenly developed a guilty conscience?" she wondered. "Perhaps I'm nearing my menopause. I know that my girls are well looked after. They lack for nothing and can even put by a 'nest egg' for their old age. They are subjected to frequent medical check-ups and the clients we have are all respectable and high up on the social ladder. So why am I getting these twinges of guilt?"

She looked up at the girls again. Three of them would be pliant. They would be obedient and comply with the rules. But the fourth showed a stubborn streak, which would have to be subdued with a great deal of tact.

"She's about the same age as my daughter Meghna – my sweet innocent child tucked away in a boarding school far away. It's the saddest part of my life being separated from her. This is the sacrifice I have to make for the life I'm leading. Hope she'll have it in her heart to think kindly of me some day."

Madam noticed that Nimmo had worn her own clothes. She had tucked the end of her *pallav* into her waistband. The dark colour of her sari highlighted her fair complexion. Her hair was combed back and neatly plaited, with a pink ribbon at its end. A thin nose ring hung from the bridge of her nose, and a yellow bead chain dangled from her neck. She had not forgotten the red dot on her forehead.

Madam observed that she had a healthy appetite. She ate daintily unlike the others who stuffed their mouths with *chapatti* and *sabzi.*

"So, how many of you can speak Hindi or English?" Madam asked.

"We speak broken Hindi," one of them said, "but we understand the language well. None of us can speak English."

"I can," Nimmo confessed, "Gregory Sahib for whom I cooked and cleaned, taught me Hindi and English. I'm not very good at either. But I think I can make myself understood."

"Who is this Gregory Sahib? Why did you have to cook and clean for him?"

"He's a writer and he lives in a small cottage in our village. He paid me well for the work. As an extra bonus, he taught me and my siblings how to read and write. He even regaled us with the stories he had written. If we liked them, he would send them to be printed in some book.

I could not even tell him I was leaving as he had gone to Delhi for some work."

Madam Aum had no intention of rushing the girls.

"They need acclimatization and then a period of motivation or rather brainwashing – glimpses into the high life they can lead if they cooperate and learn how to please. Money corrupts like nothing else. These girls have only seen poverty so far. They must crave for the good things of life. Only then will they be motivated to work."

A lazy week went by. Except for the embarrassing striptease before the lady doctor which was mandatory and a series of blood tests, life was one big holiday. They were given good food, new clothes and toiletry.

"I want you to put away the bundles you brought from home in the store room. You're free to collect them when you go back to your villages."

Nimmo refused to give up her patchwork quilt. "I cannot sleep without it. I've used it since the day it was completed."

"Silly!" said Madam, "I've given you a beautiful bedspread. Must you hang on to that rag?"

"It's precious to me. I've collected those bits of cloth and spent hours working on it in my spare time."

"Suit yourself then. But if I find any lice or bed bugs, you can bet I'll have it burnt."

"I'm not used to sitting idle. When do I begin work? What are the jobs I'm supposed to do?" Nimmo asked.

"You'll have plenty of work to do in a little while. So don't be in a hurry. Enjoy yourself and watch all those videos I've left in your room. The house keeper will come and show you how to play them."

The girls had never seen such scandalous films before. They hemmed and hawed and hid their faces. Then curiosity got the better of them and they couldn't take their eyes off the screen. By now, they had caught glimpses of the residents of the first and second floors who dressed and talked like the girls in the videos. But Madam had warned that there must be no communication with them.

"They are hard workers and in need of their rest. So don't go knocking on their doors. Make as little noise as possible."

The door of their floor was always locked at night when the lower floors came to life. Peeping through the windows, they saw fancy cars pull up the gate and well-dressed individuals entering. Sometimes Madam's voice could be heard welcoming them.

It took almost a month for the happy life to lose its sheen. Madam talked to them collectively at first, then individually. Now she didn't soft pedal her words.

"I'm in the entertainment business. My job is to find girls who will please the men who come looking for fun. Some have marital problems, some are lonely, some want a night or two of fun. They are good and respectable people, looking for a brief respite from their responsibilities. They pay well for confidentiality. They are generous with tips if satisfied. All you have to do is be good to them and do what they ask. But sometimes, a troublesome person may come along. If you bring it to my notice, that person will never be allowed in again."

"We were told it would be domestic work," protested Nimmo. "That is the only reason my parents sent me here. Ram Ghising assured them I would be safe and had nothing to fear."

"You have nothing to fear and the income is good. You can't complain."

"And if I refuse?"

"The consequences will be serious. Do you know what it means to be starved?"

"Oh yes! We've often lived on very little food in winter."

"Then perhaps you haven't heard of flogging."

Nimmo's face turned an angry red.

"And I thought you were a good woman wanting to help poor girls support their families."

"That's exactly what I'm doing. Once you get the taste of this life, you'll be hankering for more."

"Like you?"

Madam's hand made a frightful impact on Nimmo's cheek. The other girls hid their faces. Nimmo glared at the woman. Her eyes were dry though the slap hurt badly.

"I don't care what you do to me. I may be poor but I'm not about to sell myself. Someday I want to get married and have a family."

Madam waved them out of the room.

As they went up to their room, a door on the first floor opened. A sleepy woman with hair tousled called out, "Welcome to Hell! There's no escape."

Nimmo decided it would be wiser to change her tactics. A show of compliance would be better than confrontation.

Gregory Sahib was back in Nepal after a visit to his publishers in Delhi. He couldn't wait to share his excitement with his young friends.

"My sixth book is to be published and it calls for a celebration. I will take my young friends to see "Jungle Book," which is showing at the Cinema in town. I saw the posters on the hoardings, as I travelled back. Then I'll treat them to a hearty meal at the 'Dil Khush' restaurant."

He waited for Nimmo and her siblings to arrive, but there was no sign of them.

"Perhaps they think I'm still in Delhi. I'll surprise them with a visit to their hut."

While he was still some distance away, the children rushed to meet him.

"Our Nimmo has gone to Bombay," they said sadly, "We miss her very much. Who knows when she'll be back?"

"What? Gone to Bombay? Who sent her there? Come let me talk to your parents."

His anxiety propelled him towards the hut.

Nimmo's mother rushed out.

'What has brought Gregory Sahib here?' she wondered.

But when she saw the scowl on his face, she called out to her husband.

Without the customary greeting he asked, "Where have you sent Nimmo? And with whom?"

"She has got a good job in the city, Sahib. We have already been given an advance of five thousand rupees. Ram Ghising is a good man. He said he is an officer in some government department which helps poor people. He has got jobs for four girls from our village."

"You ignorant fools! How could you sell your daughter to a stranger?"

"He said he'll come again in two months' time with her salary. Nimmo is working for a rich lady."

"You have no idea where our young Nepali girls land up," Gregory Sahib scolded, "Do you have this man's address? Or the address of the rich lady Nimmo is working for? You are plain greedy. You'll never see your daughter again."

With that, he walked off in the direction of town.

Instances of trafficking of Nepali girls had been hitting the headlines regularly. This incident would have to be brought to the notice of the social welfare authorities as well as the police. The girls were all minors.

Gregory D'Mello was a middle- aged writer who had lived in the hills for over two decades. He had come here as a young man to pursue his writing in peace and had never left. The mountains had cast their spell on him and the simple rural people had welcomed him with open arms. Now they were his people and the village was his permanent home. Occasionally he would go down to Delhi or Calcutta to see about the publication of his books. He was something of a publisher's nightmare, as he refused to actively involve himself in the promotion of his books.

"No fancy reading in five star hotels. No promotional tours all over the country. I will not sit like a frog on a rock 'croaking to an admiring bog.' I can't remember which poet said that."

He was comfortable in the company of children and loved to relate his stories to them. He was the village's Pied Piper.

Gregory Sahib visited the huts of the other three girls who had gone with Nimmo and berated their parents just as harshly as he had done to Nimmo's. Now they were truly worried. Would they ever see their daughters again?

"The Sahib says that our daughters will be used by many men. They might even contract illness and die. As for their wages, Ram Ghising will take it all away. It is dreadful and frightening to have endangered our dear daughters so."

Gregory Sahib had stirred up a hornet's nest and the villagers were beside themselves. How would they contact Ram Ghising? They knew nothing about the man. But the writer had started the ball rolling. The police would be on the lookout for him.

"He will surface in some other part of Nepal," said the Police Inspector, "Greed sometimes makes one careless. They say that the going rates for young virgins sent to Bombay is Rs. 25,000. He would have made a neat lakh on the four girls from your village."

Gregory turned away sadly. He knew Nimmo from her childhood. She used to accompany her mother who worked for him. She had grown into a lovely teenager and had been cooking and cleaning for him for the last three years when her mother couldn't cope anymore. She was always cheerful, and knew how to keep her siblings happy in spite of their many deprivations.

"I must find her," Gregory thought, "the young ones look so sad and lost without her."

The room that Nimmo was pushed into a few days later was on the ground floor. It was not too far from Madam's room. Madam was not taken in by Nimmo's docility. This would be her first night of employment, and if she gave trouble, Madam could quickly intervene. She had scaled down her own activities these days unless they were very special customers. So on most nights, she was free to have a good night's sleep.

Nimmo had smuggled her quilt into the new room assigned to her. It was a sort of crutch that she believed would see her through the ordeal. She had also brought her money pouch along. The ground floor rooms were reserved for very special people. They paid extra for privacy and could come in through a secret corridor on to which the back doors of the rooms opened. There was no way that one customer would bump into another as they were slotted efficiently and time spans didn't overlap. Madam's management techniques could never be faulted.

The man who came through the door was young and nervous. He was probably about twenty-five. He gave her a timid smile and Nimmo relaxed. She had come prepared for assault, imagining that her first customer would be a prosperous middle-aged man – something like a wrestler, who would pound her into a pulp if she didn't acquiesce. She had even planned out her strategy carefully.

"I'll go into a trance like I've seen the witches do in my village. I'll pretend to be possessed by the Devi and flail my arms and legs around. No one will dare touch a Devi. And if that doesn't work, I still have another trick up my sleeve."

She pulled out the piece of mirror she had brought from home. It was like a triangle, but one point was larger and sharper than the other sides. In her village, she used to preen herself before it. Now she had made a hole in the quilt and secreted it there. One jab into the neck would settle the man forever. She had seen her father kill chickens by slitting their throats and she was confident she could do the same.

"But this boy seems too easy to handle. I can beat him if there's a scuffle, but I think he's pretty harmless. However, I must not underestimate him. He could make such a noise that Madam would come rushing in. No, I must use my cunning to threaten him and make him consent to do what I say."

"Sit down," she said, indicating one end of the bed. "Shall I pour you a drink?"

Madam had told them that it would be good to get the customers drunk just a little.

"Oh no!" the young man said, "I don't touch alcohol."

"Tell me why have you come here?" she asked.

"Isn't it obvious? This is supposed to be a house of pleasure." He grinned nervously.

Nimmo slowly brought out the piece of mirror from its hiding place. She rubbed the pointed edge of it on her palm, just like she had seen the village barber do with his shaving knife.

"Put that thing away," he said nervously. "I mean no harm to you. In fact, this is my first visit to a place like this. My friends thought such an experience would be good for my physique. I won't make any abnormal demands - just the usual routine you know. Do you always threaten your customers and chase them away?"

She glared angrily at him.

"Then I'd better leave."

"Sit down. You can't leave just as yet. I'm sure Madam has already been paid for the night. I know she collects her dues in advance."

"Yes, the payment was sent last evening."

"Then you can't run away without putting me into trouble," she said, once again sliding the mirror across her palm. "You can lie down for a while if you like. The bed is freshly made."

"No thank you. I'd rather sit," he said, indicating a stool in the corner.

"Listen carefully," Nimmo said, now that she was truly in command of the situation. God had heard her prayers and sent this boy who was not only inexperienced but scared.

"When you go out in the wee hours by the secret corridor, you will take me with you. No customer leaves that early. So we won't be seen. All you have to do is get me out of this hell before anything happens to me. The next customer may be a seasoned visitor. I promise I won't bother you after that."

"Okay," he said, "but put that darned shard away."

His car was parked a little distance away, in a quiet lane. Even the stray dogs seemed to have gone to sleep.

"Get in the back and keep your head down," he cautioned.

When they had driven some distance she said, "I'll get off now."

"No you won't, unless you want to end up in a worse place than Madam's. Only women with loose character roam about at night. You can stay in my house till morning. Then you decide what you want to do."

"You won't go to the police, will you?" she asked nervously.

Now that the tables had turned, he was bolder.

"Don't talk anymore. I've had enough for one night."

"This man is a magician," thought Nimmo, "His gate opens automatically when he approaches. Even the garage door rises to let his car in."

She didn't know he could regulate these things with the touch of a button.

"Do you live here alone? Oh my God! Serves me right for believing you."

"Shut up girl. You'll wake up the whole neighbourhood. You're quite safe here."

He showed her one of the spare bedrooms.

"Lock yourself in," he said gruffly.

Rahul Chinnappa paced his room all night. He knew he had bought himself a packet of trouble. He was a rich guy with no encumbrances. He worked in the IT city and carried home a hefty salary. He worked hard, lived well and spent lavishly. His clique of like-minded friends was just as party loving and extravagant. He was the butt end of all their jokes because he never had a girlfriend.

"Hey, something must be wrong with you. While we have been changing girls as frequently as we change our clothing, you haven't so much as held a girl's hands."

"And you're the handsomest guy among us all. There are a string of pretty women waiting to fall into your arms. What's wrong with you *yaar*?"

"Something's not in order. Do you think what I think?" said one mischievous guy.

"Stop it fellows," said Rahul irritably, "When the right girl comes along, I'll know."

Their banter had gone on for several months and Rahul began to wonder if he was abnormal. After the last party, they gave him an ultimatum.

"We are your friends, Rahul. If you're gay, why pretend otherwise?"

He was really mad now. "How can I prove to you that I'm not different?"

"Look, we don't have to wait till a girl drops into your lap. Madam Aum has the best line-up of girls. I've been there on and off myself and can assure you that they are all young and pretty. Besides, Madam assures her clients of confidentiality. But she always asks for advance payment. If you dare take up the challenge, I'll make the payment. Consider it my contribution. You've got to prove to us and to yourself that you are straight," said Yadav.

And that's how Rahul had ended up in the den of iniquity.

Now, he was even more uncertain about his sexual orientation.

"Perhaps what they say about me is true. I just didn't feel any desire to touch the girl. A real spitfire there – threatening me with that broken mirror! Of course I could have overpowered her. But the very thought of contact made me nervous. I felt like Holden Caulfield in 'The Catcher in the Rye,' on his first visit to a prostitute. He was so nervous, he could only sit in the room and make small talk. And like him, I'll have to tell my friends that it was an awesome experience. Otherwise they'll either rag me to death or despise me."

He must have fallen asleep towards morning. But he got up with a start to the clanging of the gate. His man Friday had arrived.

"Ramu will think I've been sleeping with the girl. But who cares? Every young man has a fling once in a while."

Nimmo waited until she heard Rahul's door open. Then she rushed out into the passage and dropped at his feet.

"Please don't send me away as yet. Just help me write a letter to Gregory Sahib. I'll beg him to come and take me home. Till then, let me stay. I'll do all the chores in your house, and I promise I won't be any trouble."

Those eyes implored him to be kind. Gone was her resentment of the night before. Now she looked desperate and frightened. Rahul put his hands on her shoulders and gently lifted her up.

"You're safe here. Stay as long as you like and nobody will bother you. I'll help you send off that letter. And who is Gregory Sahib?"

"He's the man for whom I cook and clean. He's a writer and a very kind man. He'll surely come and take me home."

"Don't you have parents?"

"I have, but they have never been out of our village and are too poor to come all the way."

Rahul was touched by her story. The tension of the previous night had vanished and he felt no animosity towards her. Though she had left him no choice, he had rescued her from a degrading profession. Now he felt responsible to see her through this difficult time and send her back to her parents.

"Let's have breakfast. Then we shall write the letter to your Sahib."

He watched her as she tackled her plate of *dosais* hot from Ramu's griddle and gulp down her tea.

"Haven't eaten since last morning," she said, "I was under so much tension, planning my escape. I couldn't confide in anyone. Just kept praying that the customer who came to my room would be a good man."

She looked up at him and blushed.

"I'm sorry I threatened you with my piece of mirror. I was just desperate to save myself."

"You don't know how lucky you are," thought Rahul, "If it was any of my friends, that piece of mirror couldn't have deterred them."

He noticed that she was pretty in her own way. The smoothness of her skin reflected the freshness of the hills. She had brown cornea that looked out from below slanting eyes.

Rahul couldn't help staring. He had never worked up enough courage to look closely into a girl's face. He had been extremely shy. But now contrary to his fears, something began to stir within him.

"I want to reach out and hold her hands. I want to assure her of my help. Perhaps I'm not different after all. Just a late starter."

Gregory D'Mello's complaint to the police had set the ball rolling. The Bombay police had been alerted. But searching for Ram Ghising was like looking for a grain of mustard in a sackful of paddy. The number of procurers and pimps in Bombay alone ran into thousands. Many in the law-enforcing agency had been bought off by these offenders.

But Ram Ghising had turned too ambitious and too greedy. In just over a month, he surfaced again at another village, a long way from Nimmo's home. As he re-entered India with three new captives, the police pounced on him.

"I'm just a social worker," argued Ram, "I'm doing a service to poor families by finding their daughters jobs as domestic helps. They earn a good salary and are cared for well."

There were many questions to which he could not give convincing answers and turned evasive. In the end, he broke down and confessed. He also gave them the address of Madam Aum's establishment.

When Inspector Dharam knocked on Madam Aum's door, he went alone without his posse of policemen. Madam's eyes registered anxiety. She turned her flushed face to his and asked, "Dharam, is something the matter with the girl......Meghna?"

"No."

"Then why have you come? I haven't seen you in years. Surely this is not a social visit."

"Be quiet for a while," he said, looking at the face he had once loved. She was still beautiful, and though she had put on some weight, she looked comely.

"You need not worry about Meghna. For all practical purposes she is dead to you. I have warned you and the warning still stands. If you make any attempt to contact her, I will ruin you. I will not allow her life to be besmirched by your character."

Dharam had courted her for almost a year. When he knew she was pregnant, he offered her marriage. But she had spurned him as if he were a stray mongrel.

"I'm not going to compound my mistake by marrying a constable. I want someone who will provide me with a rich and comfortable life."

She was young and haughty then and the very thought of being tied down to a policeman horrified her. When the child was born, she had gladly parted with her and Dharam made sure that Meghna was legally his. Years later, when she attempted to claim her rights, Dharam got a restraining order from the court on the basis of her character and profession.

"Tell me," she said again.

"A girl called Nimmo was brought here by a man called Ram Ghising. Where is she? She is a minor and her parents want her back. You know the type of punishment you can get for employing underage girls."

Madam Aum wrung her hands.

"I don't know where she is. She ran away from here, probably with a client."

"Let's have his name."

"That's confidential. I cannot reveal any names."

"You cannot suppress information. I could always get a court order."

"I cannot betray the confidence of a client."

"Then we will have to close the place down, as I'm sure half your girls are underage."

"Dharam, don't let your anger against me prejudice your decisions."

"May I remind you Madam Aum, that you are addressing Inspector Dharam. I must trace the girl. If you don't disclose the name of the client who took the girl away, then I must come back with a search warrant."

"You are cruel," she said, "And I thought you were a good man."

Reluctantly, she gave him the name of the man who had sent her the money. His name was Yadav Rao. She hoped it would not cause him too much embarrassment.

When Inspector Dharam knocked on Yadav's doors early that evening, it was locked.

"These rich young boys use their apartments only to sleep," he thought, "Most of their leisure hours are spent either at a pub or a club."

He tracked Yadav down to the Bombay Gymkhana, where the friends usually met for dinner. Rahul had not yet put in an appearance.

Inspector Dharam took Yadav aside. He wanted information about the missing girl.

"Missing girl? Good Heavens! Why would I kidnap a girl?"

Then he remembered and let out a loud guffaw.

"Did Madam Aum give you my name? There must be some mistake. I came to the club straight from my office and was here till the wee hours. We were playing billiards," he said, pointing to his friends. "You can go to the manager and look up the records. Check when I signed out of here. Perhaps you should search Madam Aum's apartment. She could be hiding the girl there. Besides, I don't have to go to such a place. I have my reputation to think about."

When Inspector Dharam left, the friends discussed the matter.

"Rahul has not only visited Madam Aum's establishment, he has even kidnapped the girl. So he's not that effeminate after all. In fact, he's quite a dark horse. He never said a word to any of us."

"He's been acting strange lately - not frequenting the club as he used to. Says he's very busy at work. Perhaps we should pay him a surprise visit tonight."

"Give him a break yaar. Let him enjoy himself. He's a late starter, but boy... isn't he catching up fast!"

Reluctant to leave Nimmo alone for long periods, Rahul began to pay just a token visit to the club and then rush home for dinner. When Yadav had asked if he had enjoyed his visit to Madam Aum, Rahul had merely nodded. Now Yadav was curious to find out more.

"Hold it Rahul. You're in a mighty hurry these days. Tell me what's going on. Inspector Dharam was here a while ago. He says that Madam Aum has reported the abduction of one of her employees."

Rahul paled. If the police were on the lookout for her, then it would not be long before she was traced. And he would be implicated.

"You look kind of sick, man. What's the matter? Tell me. I'm your friend, I can help."

Rahul told him the whole story.

"There's no hanky panky between us. She's just waiting for someone to come and take her home. If as you say, you're my good friend – remember you got me into this mess in the first place – then cover up for me with the others. She's pretty bored at home doing nothing. My servant objects to her pottering around in his domain."

Nimmo paced the floor endlessly. Time hung heavy on her hands and it made her restless. All she could think of was getting back to the security of her home. How long would it take for Gregory Sahib to receive her letter? Would he come to fetch her immediately? Would he really be bothered about her welfare? After all, he was only her employer and might have found a replacement by now.

Though Rahul could understand her anxiety, there was little he could do to mitigate her fear and loneliness. Yadav had spread the word that Rahul had a house guest and therefore couldn't spend much time at the club.

"How long is she staying?" asked his friends.

"Till she's fed up," he said, and didn't volunteer any information.

Though they had nothing in common to talk about, his very presence in the house gave Nimmo comfort. The servant Ramu was unfriendly.

"The master says you are his guest, so you better relax and enjoy his hospitality," he said, plying her with tea and biscuits at frequent intervals and loading her plate with rice at lunch time.

"Turn on the TV," Rahul urged, "There are some good programmes. Perhaps that will take your mind off your troubles."

"But how long can I stay here?"

"Until someone comes to take you home," he consoled. "You are safe here. But if you want to go back to Madam Aum's, I could send you there."

"No, no, I just want to go home." Tears threatened to spill over again.

He was getting used to her presence in the house and he knew he would miss her when she was gone.

He found her sobbing bitterly one evening.

"It's two months to the day and no one has come to take me back."

Instinctively, he put his arm around her shoulders and she clung to him and sobbed against his chest.

"Don't cry," he said, "You just tell me the name of your village and I'll find out how to get there. I could accompany you home."

"Will you really? Promise?"

"I will," Rahul said, drawing her closer.

For him, this was a moment of discovery. He loved the feeling of her proximity, the softness of her skin, the fresh fragrance of the soap she used. And he knew without a doubt that he was a normal young man. Just a late developer, more so because of his innate shyness.

Gregory D'Mello arrived as soon as he could. He was in his early sixties – a plump Santa Claus-like figure with chubby cheeks and curly white hair.

"Sahib, you have come!" Nimmo cried, falling over him as if he were her long lost father.

It was a touching sight.

"My girl, I've missed you. There's no one who can cook a meal for me like you do. Tell me everything. Begin from the time you left the village."

Rahul watched them as she recited her story.

"A narrow escape, my girl! And if this young man hadn't come along, who knows what might have happened!"

"Are you a relative?" Rahul asked timidly. "Or perhaps her sugar daddy!"

"Get off with you," Gregory Sahib replied, "I'm father to all the little children in the village. I have no family other than these children. And don't you be so wicked as to assume otherwise. By the same token, I could ask you if you've played fast and loose with her. If you have, I'll gladly take my hatchet to your throat."

Nimmo looked from one to the other, suddenly afraid that they were having a fight.

"No, no," she said, pushing them apart.

"We'll be leaving early tomorrow. If you'll be so kind as to give me a bed for the night, I'll be grateful," said Gregory.

When they said their farewells the next day, Rahul felt a strange emptiness.

"She's like a pink magnolia that grows only in the mountains," said Gregory, "She will never survive in the plains."

They had done each other a reciprocal service. While he had rescued Nimmo from Madam Aum's clutches, she had helped him restore faith in his own manhood.

"Pink Magnolia, did he say? Perhaps I'll soon find one that blossoms in the plains."

GATEWAY'S SINGING SENSATION

An awful feeling of guilt swept over me. I had never experienced such an emotion before. Life had always been one long struggle for survival, and it didn't bother me on whose feet I trod. But this was different. I had betrayed a good lady's faith in me. Mrs. Meher Irani was special. She had picked me off the streets seven months ago, when I lay moaning and groaning on a pavement in Colaba. I had a raging fever for almost three days.

"Hey girl, why are you lying on the streets? Don't you have a home? No parents?"

I was too ill to answer.

"Dear God! You're burning with fever. You'll die if you don't get some treatment. I'm taking you to the hospital."

The lady lifted me up in spite of my stinking clothes and led me to her car. Then she drove me to the nearest municipal hospital.

"Go call the duty doctor," she told the nurse, "I'm not leaving till he has examined her."

The doctor took his own time coming.

"Aren't you the duty doctor?" she asked, "You should have come at once. This girl is going to have fits if her temperature doesn't come down soon."

"Madam, why are you so agitated?"

He took one look at me. "From which dustbin have you picked her up? She's not a VIP, is she?"

Mrs. Irani didn't raise her voice. But what she said galvanized him into action.

"Sorry Ma'am," he said, "I'll do my best. Please don't create problems for me."

She waited until I was wheeled out of the ward and put in a clean bed.

"Take good care of her," she told the nurses, "and call the doctor if the temperature doesn't subside. I'll be back tomorrow."

Dressed in a clean hospital gown with my hair combed back and plaited, I must have looked respectable.

"Who would have thought you were so pretty under all that dirt and grime? The colour seems to have come back to your cheeks," she said. "You'll be discharged in a day or two. Now tell me where you live. I'll contact your parents and ask them to take you home."

"I have no parents and no home. For as long as I can remember, the streets have been my home. I sleep in the open corridor of the Colaba shopping area, not far from where you found me. You could leave me there."

"But you're too weak to go back to the streets just now." She was silent for a while. "I'll take you home for the present. You can rest in the gardener's tool shed until you get back your strength."

I was in no condition to refuse.

"Thank you Ma'am, I'm very grateful."

I recovered my strength and my spirits within a few days. I knew the gardener didn't like my presence in the tool shed.

"Nuisance," he grumbled, "Why must Madam give shelter to every stray that comes along? You look strong enough to me. You should think of leaving."

Had I been really strong I would have given him some lip and used my choicest swear words. But after his initial opposition, he began to tolerate my presence.

"Come into the garden instead of lying on your mat all day. The fresh air will do you good. See how beautiful my roses are. But don't you dare touch the flowers. Just look, smell and enjoy. If I catch you pulling at the petals, I'll have Madam drive you away."

But when the time came for me to leave, he was sad.

"Why don't you ask Madam to employ you? You could make yourself useful by doing some household chores. She'll pay you well."

Mrs. Irani too was reluctant to let me go.

"You're too young to be roaming the streets. It's not safe. Tell me about yourself. Are there any relatives with whom you could stay?"

"No. They said I was a burden to them though I worked all day for my keep. Sometimes I was starved and many times, whipped. So I ran away to the railway station and got into a train. There were urchins like me who rode the trains. They taught me how to beg with dignity," I laughed.

"There is no dignity in begging," she said sternly.

"I was working in exchange for money. That's not exactly begging."

People in the compartments threw papers, food or banana skins. Some spat on the floor, others blew their noses and wiped their dirty fingers on the benches. The railway coolies didn't bother to clean the coaches. One of the urchins lent me a brush and a rag. I began cleaning the floors and demanding money from the passengers. Many would abuse and chase me away. But there were good people who gave generously and even offered food.

For a few months, I shuttled back and forth on the trains. At night, I slept in an empty bogie of any train parked at the siding. I was happy. No one to scold or beat me. I was better off than living with relatives.

Then one day, a passenger thrust a bag of fruits into my hands. I was busy peeling an orange in the passage near the toilet when police arrived with sniffer dogs. They went straight for my bag of fruits. I never knew that at the bottom of the bag there was something the police were searching for.

"Come with us," the policeman said as he tweaked my ear and dragged me out of the compartment.

"I didn't steal it," I shouted, "I swear in the name of all the gods that I'm not a thief."

"Shut up and come along. So this is what you do on the train – peddle drugs? Who is your boss? Just give us his name."

"I swear the bag doesn't belong to me. I don't have a boss. I only clean the floor of the carriages and ask for money. That's how I support myself."

But the cops kept me in the lock-up for three days and beat me several times until I thought I would die. Then they chased me out with a warning never to get back on the train again. So there I was, alone and frightened with no place to go except the streets.

Begging was something I didn't want to do. But how could I earn my keep? I'd go to Crawford Market early in the morning and ask shoppers, especially women, whether I could carry their purchases while they shopped and take the stuff to their vehicles. Memsahibs were always in search of coolies to help them. So I made a decent income on most days. There were a few shopkeepers who employed me to sweep and swab the floors of their shops before customers arrived. This too brought in some money. So I didn't make much fuss if they sometimes squeezed my bottom or pinched my cheeks.

Mrs. Irani listened quietly to my story without interrupting.

"Now I must go back to work," I said, "If I don't work, I'll starve. You've been very good to me Ma'am. I could have died on the road like a stray dog if you hadn't taken me to the hospital and then brought me here to rest."

"Don't go," Mrs. Irani said, "You can help my maid with the housework and I'll pay you a decent salary. The streets are not safe for young girls."

This was an attractive offer and I couldn't refuse. I shifted from the tool shed to the servants' quarters. The maid Sarasu was happy for some company. She did most of the work and gave me only a few light jobs to do.

Mrs. Irani lived alone in a big house. I didn't see any signs of a husband or children. But I could guess she was a rich woman. She did a lot of social work in the community. But when she was home, the house came alive with music. No Hindi songs for her. Her favourites were Michael Jackson, Elton John, Bon Jovi and other music makers. I learnt something about these musicians from her. Just by listening to the music I picked up a few tunes and would sing along using words that sounded similar.

"Don't murder the song girl," Madam would scold, "Here, let me teach you the correct words."

I was a quick learner and she was a good teacher. She wasn't averse to shaking a leg to MJ's tunes and taught me how to dance too.

"You don't need to call yourself Appu anymore. You're like a cobra that dances to the snake charmer's flute. You can twist and wriggle like a snake. Henceforth your name will be Nagina."

I was happy in Mrs. Irani's house. I had very little work to do and plenty of good food to eat. I could sing and dance and even speak a few words of English.

"Would you like to go to school?" she asked many times.

My answer was always a vehement 'No.'

In my seventh month as Mrs. Irani's maid, she asked me to accompany her to Crawford Market for her supply of fruit and vegetables. That was the day the bug of restlessness bit me.

I saw my old street friends hanging around and badgering memsahibs for work to do. I waved to several of them through the car window, but they didn't recognize me.

"Oh for the freedom of the streets!" I thought, "Here I am trapped in a golden cage and can't run about as I used to. There are rules to be followed in Mrs. Irani's house. Why don't my friends recognize me? Do I look different or are they are afraid of Madam?"

The restless feeling stayed with me for several days. I longed for my friends and freedom. I had no one to chat with except the maid and the gardener. And though Mrs. Irani was the nicest person I ever met, I felt an aching loneliness of not being able to laugh and joke with my friends, or exchange notes at the end of the day. It was fun to smoke a *bidi* occasionally or sniff glue for the fun of it.

"I'm missing out on life," I thought, "I feel like a bird with its wings clipped. No excitement that would give me goose pimples; too many rules to follow. Bathing every day is compulsory, and the gardener refuses to give me a flower for my hair if it is not neatly combed and plaited."

I spent many sleepless nights tossing and turning in bed. In my dreams, I heard my friends calling, "Come Appu, come and join us. Look at the fun you are missing."

One day I woke up long before dawn. I was determined to run away, but I had no money. Mrs. Irani had saved all my salary in a Post Office account. But I knew she had pinned two hundred rupee notes under a vase on the dining table. It was for the milkman.

"I'll take the money. Mrs. Irani can keep all my salary."

I packed two sets of good clothing in a cloth bag, with little knick knacks I had collected over these seven months. I was out of the house while it was still dark. No one saw me leave. Then I walked as fast as I could, running over some stretches until I reached Colaba Causeway. People were still sleeping in the corridor.

"Hey, wake up," I said, nudging some and shaking the others, "Wake up! I'm back and have so much to tell you."

"Appu, why are you dressed up like that? Where are your street clothes? There are many bad men looking for pretty girls. Someone might kidnap you."

I had saved my street clothes though Mrs. Irani had asked me to throw them away.

"I'll be with you in a minute," I said, and ran behind the shops that were still closed. I quickly changed into my old *lehenga* and blouse. They were clean and smelled of Mrs. Irani's home.

I folded my good clothes and pushed them into the cloth bag. Now the problem was to keep the bag from being stolen by my mates. I put my money into a flat pouch and hung it around my neck close to my skin.

"I'll just have to dangle the bag from my shoulder until I find a place to keep it."

We were soon walking towards Crawford Market. We stopped at Dhirubhai's tea shop for a cup of tea and a *gutli*.

"Haven't seen you for months," Dhirubhai said, "Were you ill or did you find work elsewhere?"

"I was very ill and a kind lady let me stay in her tool shed until I got better and stronger."

"Good for you. But you look too clean for the streets," he smiled. "Couldn't you have found work in the lady's house?"

"I'm back among my friends again and that makes me happy. *Bhai*, can I ask you for a small favour? I want to leave my bag here until I finish work."

"It will be safe with me," he promised.

But getting back to the old lifestyle was not easy. I had lost touch with street behaviour.

I followed several women into the market.

"Madam, can I carry your basket?"

I could not bring back that maddening whine into my voice. I could not tap my stomach and cringe, "No food since yesterday, Ma'am. Give me a few rupees to carry your basket so that I can have a meal today." I would often lift up my blouse and show them how thin I was.

Now it was difficult. Even before I could approach a customer, someone would beat me to it. I had lost touch with street life and even forgotten the street lingo. By the end of the day, I had only made ten rupees while some of my friends had even collected up to hundred rupees.

"Never mind," said Dhirubhai, "You'll catch up with the others in a day or two. Here, have another *pav* with your tea. You can pay me later when you have money."

Mrs. Irani had spoilt me for the streets. How foolish I had been to give up a good life and opt for this life! I didn't realize how much I would miss the music and the songs I had learnt, the comfy mattress, the tasty food, and Mrs. Irani's cheerful laughter. I had thrown it all away for the life of a vagabond and a place on the pavement for my home.

"Oh my God!" I sighed, "What have I done? I cannot go back to Mrs. Irani after stealing her money and abusing the privileges she had given me. She would never forgive me. Perhaps she has already gone to the police about the theft. Even now they may be searching for me."

I kept tossing and turning on the hard ground that night. The girl on the right threw her legs about in her sleep and kicked me in my stomach. The one on the left talked throughout the night. The fear that someone would steal my bag made me use it as my pillow.

"Dear God, how foolish I have been! Why did I ever come back to the streets?"

In the wee hours of the morning I heard drops of water dripping from a faucet nearby. "I must finish my ablutions before the other women come with their water pots."

I jumped up and ran to the tap. No one was around. So I quickly undressed and bathed. Then I put on the same dirty street clothes. But as I was doing so I saw two eyes staring at me through the branches of a tree behind the tap.

"You filthy old man!" I screamed, and rushed back to the pavement. I was lucky he didn't run off with my bag when I was bathing.

After a week of street life and finding odd jobs to do, I felt I had endured enough. I just couldn't be a street girl anymore. What Mrs. Irani said was true. A female vagabond, whatever her age, was easy prey to wicked men. I could be raped, kidnapped or sold into prostitution or as a bonded slave to some powerful goon. I could contract all kinds of illness because of the unhealthy way I lived. Yes, she had given me at least a dozen reasons why I should forsake my old ways. I refused to listen to good advice and had come back to the rough and tumble of street life.

One night, I was squatting on the maidan with my friends for my evening natter. Some of the urchins had joined us too. They were passing around joints which we all puffed on in turns. Now it didn't seem such a jolly thing to do. I just couldn't get into the mood.

"There are better things for you than the street," I heard Mrs. Irani's voice, "Your life is what you make of it."

Then like a thunderbolt, police *lathis* whizzed through the air and landed on our backs. We scattered in different directions like frightened mice. Our only aim was to escape, and I didn't stop until I reached my safe corridor. My mind was made up. I would quit the streets and find some other occupation.

Next morning, I did not set off with the others. I headed towards the Gateway of India. It was usually deserted in the mornings. I sat down on the side facing the sea and took stock of my assets. I had two hundred stolen rupees in the pouch around my neck and two sets of decent clothing. They were my only earthly possessions. As I sat there looking out to sea, I felt as if I had been pushed into those dark waters but was struggling to surface.

"Oh God!" The words involuntarily escaped my lips. I knew nothing about God. Where was he? Where did he live? Why did he not care for me? Then something within me said, "You're not the only one with problems. Everyone has something or other to worry about. But to rise above your troubles and get on with your life, you probably need God on your side."

This was my epiphany. I remembered the words of Mrs. Irani's favourite song. She had taken the trouble to teach me the words.

"Somewhere over the rainbow way up high......... Birds fly over the rainbow, why oh why can't I?"

I felt relieved. A new strength coursed through my veins. A renewed hope for a better tomorrow wafted over me.

As I got up to leave, I saw a foreign woman approaching. What did she want? I made ready to run.

"Wait, wait," she said, "I heard someone singing here. Do you know where that person has gone?"

"There was no one here but me."

"Don't tell me you can sing like that?"

"I can and I will sing for you," I said, belting out the same song.

"Beautiful! And why are you here at this hour? Have you run away from school?"

"Never been inside a school. I can't even write my name."

"But the song – where did that come from?"

I told her about my life on the streets and the happy time I spent in Mrs. Irani's house.

"What a shame! With that voice you can go places."

"But first I must find a place to sleep. I don't want to sleep on the pavements anymore."

Martha Danby was a frequent visitor to India. She was working for an NGO that promoted the education of girls all over India.

"Come with me. I'll see what I can do," she said.

"I'm a free bird. I don't want to be confined to anybody's house. Just a place to sleep at night and keep my bag."

We were soon at the gates of an old rambling building. We had to wait for the watchman to let us in. He obviously knew Martha and greeted her.

"Is this some sort of Remand Home?" I asked. My voice was breaking up. I thought I was going to sob.

The nun who greeted us had such a grumpy face that I cried, "No, not here. This is a prison."

But Martha took hold of my hand and led me indoors and then down into the basement. It was clean and well lit, with rows of beds rolled up and resting against the wall. There was no one around.

"This is a night shelter for street children," she said, "You can come here every evening and have a bath. You'll be given your own towel and soap. They'll even give you a bun and a cup of hot soup. A clean mattress and sheet will also be provided. You can leave in the morning and no one will question you. It's free. My organization supports this project. Can you see that blue box fixed to the wall? When you can spare a few coins, put them in the box as a thank offering."

A young nun brought me a towel, soap, mattress and a sheet.

"These are yours to use. Take the last place on the left row."

She also gave me a gate pass with my name. "The watchman will let you in if you show him this."

Martha took me to a sandwich bar for lunch. I had never been inside such a place before. She saw how nervous I was.

"No one is going to object to your presence here as long as you pay the bill," she assured me.

I had watched how Mrs. Irani ate her meals so gracefully – not gobbling or chewing food noisily, but taking small bites and munching them daintily. Now I did the same hoping that Martha would be pleased with my manners.

"Now that you have found a place to sleep, what do you intend doing during the day?" she asked.

"I could become a tourist guide. I know Colaba and the Fort area like the back of my hand. I even know Crawford market and the surrounding areas. I can speak English, Hindi, and Marathi. Or I can sing and people will give me money. I learnt a few songs from Mrs. Irani.I can even dance like Michael Jackson."

Martha smiled. "Mrs. Irani must have been a good teacher. But why didn't she coax you to go to school?"

"She tried very hard. She was willing to support me through my education, but I refused. I hope you're not trying to persuade me to go to school."

"As you said, you are a free bird. I don't want to clip your wings. Do as you please if it makes you happy. Now come along. You'll need a few dresses if you want to be a tourist guide."

Martha bought me two sets of dresses and a pair of slippers. She also gave me a comb and ribbons for my hair.

"Now run along. I have a lot of work to do. Be at the Gateway tomorrow at 10 o'clock and I'll see how good a tourist guide you are."

I was there early next morning, wearing my new dress and slippers. My hair was tied up in two plaits, with ribbons to match my dress. Now the sea didn't look so treacherous anymore. I had hopes that my life would change for the better. Only the guilt of stealing Mrs. Irani's money remained. I was afraid of bumping into her someday. What would I say and how would she react?

"Are you there?"

I heard Martha's voice and turned.

"You look very pretty today. The dress fits you perfectly."

"Where shall we start?" I asked.

"At the places you know best."

So I showed her the best eating places in Colaba, the movie theatres and the expensive shops. Then I took her through the crooked *gullies* where one could haggle with the shop keepers for anything from trinkets to expensive sandalwood and ivory souvenirs, books or clothing.

"Hey Appu! Where have you been so long? We thought some foreigner had taken you away," said one shop owner.

"I'm not Appu anymore. I'm Nagina, and I'm a tourist guide now."

"Ha, ha, ha, and what will you show the tourists? The best place to buy a joint of marijuana or a grain of white powder?"

I gave him a dirty look and walked off.

"How old are you?" Martha asked.

"Who knows? May be fourteen or fifteen."

"Not a day more than ten and you're into drugs already?"

"No, no," I assured her, "I'm not a drug user, though I might have taken an occasional puff or sniffed glue for the fun of it. I can swear I didn't like it at all."

"Thank God for that."

She was not interested in the places I showed her. But she was more interested in people – the *pan masala* man with all his little tins of ingredients, the way he folded the leaves into triangular packets and pinned them in place with a clove; the food vendor with her pushcart parked at a street corner and the people flocking to buy her *idlis* and chutney or chapattis with potato *bhaji* from her gleaming stainless steel containers. Martha had so many questions to ask the lady. What time did she wake up in the morning? Did she have someone to help her? Did she have a husband and children? She liked the way the woman smiled when she counted her money after the food was all sold, tied it securely in the folds of her sari and tucked it into her waist band.

The eunuchs were scary, but she wanted to know all about them too in spite of my warning that they would fleece her for money.

At the end of the day Martha asked me what I would like to eat.

"A Frankie," I said, "I've never tasted one before as I couldn't afford the price."

"What's that?"

I led her to a shop where they were making and selling the rolls.

"Is it safe to eat?" she asked.

"Of course," I said, biting into my roll stuffed with bits of chicken.

When we parted in the evening, she put a 50-rupee note in my hand.

"You're a good tourist guide and I've learnt a lot from you. Be there tomorrow and you can take me to another area. By the way, you must behave yourself at the shelter. No quarrelling, no smoking, no drugs, or they'll throw you out."

"I'll be very good," I promised.

I was her tourist guide for a week. She loved walking and so did I. But sometimes we took a bus to save time. Martha was fascinated by the people and things that were on sale in Crawford Market. The baskets of marigold and jasmine were of particular interest, especially when she saw the women measuring lengths of flowers with their forearms. She bought me a strand of jasmine to tuck in my hair.

"Makes you smell sweet," she said.

The fisherwomen with the gathers of their saris drawn up between their legs and tucked into their waists, made her giggle.

"Real buxom rumps! Must be inviting quite a few pinches every day," she laughed, "I feel like doing it too. But they'll probably beat me to a pulp."

"That's for sure. They are 'no-nonsense' women and can deliver a solid punch if anyone gets too near."

Martha was interested in everything and everybody – the hand cart wallahs, the *dabba* wallahs, the *memsahibs* in their stylish clothes, the street acrobats! She had so many questions for me, and I was glad that I was pretty well informed, having spent my life on the streets.

"Why do you want all these details? Most tourists want to see places and take photographs. Why do you want to know about ordinary people?"

"I'm in love with Bombay and the people. I want to write about this vibrant city – the rich, the poor, the beautiful, the ugly; the castes and religions and different coloured skins, yet all so Indian."

"Will you write about me too?"

"You'll be the heroine in my book."

That evening when we sat down to have tea at a tea shop, Martha asked, "Have you enjoyed being a tourist guide?"

"It was great."

"I have to go away soon, but I want to know if you would like to come with me to my country, the USA. I've grown quite fond of you and as I have no children of my own, you can be my daughter. You must tell me by tomorrow as the procedure will take very long both in India and in my country. Perhaps the lady Mrs. Irani can help me."

"No, no. I'm too ashamed to face her. She'll probably tell you that I'm ungrateful and unreliable."

"Leave it to me," Martha said, "But you haven't given me an answer."

I was overwhelmed. "I would like to come and live in your home. Do you intend being my mama? Is there a papa too?"

"Yes," she said, "But don't build your hopes too high. The government may not allow me to adopt you."

Early next morning Martha arrived at the night shelter.

"Sister Agnes will take you to the police station. You must tell the police that you don't have parents and live on the streets. You must convince them that you are a complete orphan."

I was terrified. "No, I'm not going to the police. You never know what they'll do to me. They could lock me up for no reason."

But Martha was reassuring. "If we don't go according to the rules you will never be able to leave the country."

The nuns had a Child Adoption Agency and were familiar with the procedures. Sister Agnes dragged me to several offices before the police referred me to a Child Welfare Committee. She convinced them that I would be safe in the Catholic Adoption Agency if I was remanded to them.

"Oh my God!" I thought, "I'm going back into a cage. No, I'd rather live on the streets."

"Now you're making me angry," Martha said. "I told you there are formalities which you have to go through."

"Don't worry," Sister Agnes assured me, "If you want to continue at the night shelter you can do so and be a tourist guide by day. We won't imprison you."

Martha left the country soon after and I was lost without her. She was a loving, caring person and I was ready to follow her to the ends of the earth. I knew she would come back for me some day.

The Gateway was a good place to meet foreign tourists. Not all of them were kind. Some abused me in their native tongues – I could tell by the tone of their voices. Others shooed me off with a wave of their hands. Young people were easier to approach.

"Would you like a tour around South Bombay?" I'd ask in a business-like voice, "Souvenir buying? Cheap clothes? Food? Cinema? I know the best places."

"What about drugs?"

"Strictly no, Sir. Just places and people."

Sometimes they'd take pity on me and let me tag along with my running commentary. Sometimes they'd buy me food or thrust some money into my hands. "Thank you, you're a wonderful guide."

I could tell them the timings of the boats that left for Elephanta Caves, or give them the number of the buses plying to distant parts of Bombay. I knew the movie timings and the best places to exchange foreign money. Word got around that I was a walking information bureau and many would come and consult me.

Whenever I had no work, I'd belt out a song that I had learnt from Mrs. Irani. Most times I didn't know the meaning of the words I was singing. Sometimes even the words were not correct.

One morning I sang, "Love me for a reason.........let the reason be love."

A group formed around me, clapping and keeping time with their feet. Some took pictures of me and I posed as if born to the camera.

But a few days later, I was in for a shock. Sister Agnes called me to her office and showed me a paper with my photograph. They have called you 'The Singing Sensation of Gateway.' You've become famous. But the Child Welfare Committee is not pleased. They have accused our agency of sending you out to beg. You must be careful in future. You can jeopardize your future and also bring a bad name to our convent if you attract attention to yourself."

I thought I had a reasonably decent life. As a tourist guide I was able to support myself. Sister Agnes kept my savings with her. Many times, I put a few rupees into the blue box at the night shelter. Tourists gave me gifts of money and chocolate. Sometimes my street friends would come to see me. I would buy them food and little gifts or even lend them small amounts of money. But I was absolutely sure that I didn't want to live on the streets again.

If only I knew how to read and write! Why had I been so stubborn and refuse to go to school when Martha offered to sponsor my education?

I talked about this to Sister Agnes and she gave me some news that caused panic.

"We think you should be in foster care until all your adoption papers are ready. She has suggested the name of Mrs. Irani who is willing to take you under her wing."

"Oh no," I sighed, "I will have to run away again. I cannot face Mrs. Irani after what I've done."

Then one day, I heard a familiar voice calling, "Wait Nagina, I must talk to you. You must stay with me until your adoption papers come through."

All I could think of was the money I had stolen.

"I'm sorry Madam," I said, bending to touch her feet, "I stole that money from your house because I wanted to run away."

"Don't worry, child. Your salary for six months is still with me. I will teach you English and also how to read and write. You can't go to the States without even knowing how to sign your name."

"Thank you, Ma'am. Now that you're not angry with me, I'll gladly come. But I'm too old to learn."

"Nonsense! You can learn even if you are ninety."

Mrs. Irani became my friend, mentor and teacher. She soon got me interested in reading and writing. It was not easy. I didn't have the kind of discipline to sit down and pour over the alphabet. But with a lot of encouragement and generous incentives, I learnt to write and spell simple words.

Now when I went out, I'd look at every billboard and advertisement, spell out the alphabets and string them together until I could pronounce a word.

I also learned some new songs from Mrs. Irani, and danced to some happy tunes. Watching the way she talked and behaved, I learnt how to walk and talk like a lady. But there were times when Madam's happy mask dropped. Then I would see the pain in her eyes. Was it loneliness? Was it fear? Dared I throw my arms around her and ask what was bothering her?

When I had given up all hope of seeing Martha again, Sister Agnes asked me to come to the convent with Mrs. Irani. And there was Martha welcoming me with a big hug.

"Good news for you Nagina . The road is almost clear for your adoption into my family – yes, as my daughter. But we have to make a few visits to the courts to complete formalities."

I was overjoyed. At last I would have a mother and a father. This time, Martha's husband had come along too. He was as kind and friendly as she was.

I don't know how news of my adoption reached the media. The papers read,

"Singing Sensation of Gateway to be adopted by American couple."

I was suddenly a very busy person. Men and women with cameras came asking a lot of questions. I didn't know who they were and why they were interested in my life. But all this excitement made me talk too much. Then my face appeared in several newspapers.

"Great getaway for humble singer!"

Martha and her husband had taken me to the court to be questioned by the judge. The compound was packed with flag-wielding women. They shouted, "Go home Yankees. Down with girl-trafficking. Leave our girls alone."

I didn't know what they were saying. But when the frenzied crowd moved in on us, I became protective, lashing out at them in my gutter language which I thought I had forgotten. I hit out at everyone who came too close.

"Spitfire," they shouted, "Why should we bother about you? You can go to hell for all we care."

I was totally confused. What was all this about? Why were they angry with this kind couple who wanted to give me a home?

"They are child activists," Martha whispered, "They think we are bad people who want to take you away and destroy your life."

There were many black-coated men inside the court room. But there was one, more ferocious than the others. He was shouting at the top of his voice until the judge ticked him off. "Lower your volume please. No one is deaf here."

"I want the world to know how foreigners come to India and spirit off innocent children. They are either treated like servants or used as child prostitutes and fall easy prey to paedophiles. No self-respecting country should allow this. I move that you dismiss the plea for adoption."

I hid my face against Martha's chest.

"I have studied the case well and carefully scrutinized the antecedents of the adoptive parents. But since you have challenged the adoption, I request you to bring one couple from among your clients, who are willing to adopt Nagina legally and give her all the rights she will be entitled to. They'll be given preference over the foreign couple. I'll want you back here by 10 a.m. tomorrow. For now, the court is adjourned."

I saw the disappointment on the faces of Martha and Ross.

"We have waited for more than a year and followed the law at every stage. Why must there be last minute hitches?"

We quietly walked out of the court with the activists on our heels, waving their flags and shouting at us.

Next morning, we were in the court room on the dot of 10 a.m. But the lawyer for the activists was not there, neither were the yelling crowds. They had all vanished.

"Now I have really called off their bluff," said the judge to our lawyer.

"Is your name Nagina?" He pointed at me.

"Yes, Your Honour." The lawyer had taught me how to show respect.

"Do you want to be adopted into the family of Martha and Ross Danby?"

"I do."

He once again checked all the details recorded on my papers. Then he signed with a flourish.

"From now on you are Nagina Danby."

Martha and Ross moved forward and hugged me.

"Take good care of her," he said.

"We will, Your Honour."

There was still the job of getting my passport. That would take a few more days. I moved from Mrs. Irani's house to the International YWCA where Martha and Ross were staying. I was nervous. Living in close proximity with them would reveal all my flaws. Would they still like me? I had to visit Mrs. Irani and talk to her. She would allay all my fears.

A strange man was sitting in her porch. I had never seen him before. Even before I could open the door and enter he yelled, "Who the hell are you? How dare you walk into my garden?"

His large red eyes burrowed into me. My teeth began chattering. This wild looking man was ready to jump down from his chair and come after me.

"I want to see Mrs. Irani," I said.

"What did you say?" he bellowed.

By then, the dear lady came running out.

"Hullo Nagina! Come here."

I ran up to her, feeling the man's eyes pierce my back.

When we were indoors she said, "He's my husband. He was in the mental asylum for many years. I don't know if he escaped or was released. But he found his way home alright and the institution didn't even bother to inform me."

I saw that her face was badly bruised on the left side. There were bruises on her arms too.

"He did this to you?"

"Yes. I have to send him back somehow."

Then all of a sudden he was there, tugging at my hair and trying to lift me up. I screamed with all my might.

"Leave her alone," she shouted.

"Don't interfere, you bitch," he yelled back, swinging a blow at Mrs. Irani. I don't know from where I got the strength. As he was grappling with her, I lifted the wooden chair close by and brought it down on his head. He fell with a thud.

"Run," Mrs. Irani said, "I don't want you to get involved. You'll be leaving the country in a few days. So I don't want you to be held back for questioning. Go," she said, giving me a hug, "And may God go with you."

My legs were trembling. I took a bus back to the YWCA. Martha saw the state I was in. "I'm not leaving you out of my sight until we have all your documents and passport in hand and we are airborne."

I thought of Mrs. Irani often. Had I killed the man and let her take the blame? I did not come back to India for ten long years.

The period of adjustment to my new environment was daunting. But there was no place to run. I wasn't good at studies. So Martha admitted me to a school where I had my voice trained. Now I'm a singer with a local band.

But sometimes when I get homesick, I sing the old songs that Mrs. Irani taught me, and my heart goes out to her. She gave me so much love in spite of her own tragedy of having a mad husband.

Our band would be performing in some of the major cities in India. Bombay had now become Mumbai. So much had changed in this city that I loved. It was not a friendly place anymore. I felt the tension in the air – anger, fear, sadness or struggle reflected in the eyes of the people and their suspicious glances at strangers.

The lead guitarist was my fiancé. I gave him a tour of all the places that I had once haunted and took him to the unforgettable Gateway. I searched for my street friends but could only recognize one. She looked like a typical Marathi housewife, her head covered with her *pallav* and with a baby on her hips. She had married an auto rickshaw driver and he took good care of her. Most of the boys had melted into the underworld. Some had grown rich by taking to crime. The girls too had moved to different parts of the state, through legal or live-in relationships.

"I'm lucky to have escaped the streets," I thought, "Martha had told me a hundred times that it was only through God's grace."

I was nervous about visiting Mrs. Irani. Would she be at home or would she be behind bars? I was sure that I had killed her husband and she had taken the rap for my crime.

But there she was, reclining in an old armchair in her garden. Her hair had turned grey, and her shoulders were hunched. She wore spectacles now.

Standing a few yards away I sang, "I just called to say I love you……"

"Nagina! What a pleasant surprise to see you again! You've grown into a pretty lady."

"Tell me your news Ma'am. Did I kill your husband? I expected to see you behind bars."

"No, he didn't die. They took him back to the Institution. But mercifully, he died a year later and I was free at last."

"How could you sing and dance in spite of all your troubles?" I asked.

"God gives us the resources to cope and I think I did very well. Luckily my husband was a wealthy man and I could live in style. So now you see why I couldn't abandon him and plunge into another relationship."

"Madam, you're a saint. I don't know how many others like me you have helped."

"Let not your left hand know what your right hand is doing," she laughed.

"Meet my fiancé Tony," I said. I had quite forgotten that he was standing behind me. "He's the lead guitarist in our band."

She smiled and stretched out her hand. But Tony embraced her with one big hug.

"I've heard so much about you that I feel I know you so well. You helped Nagina so much and taught her to use her voice. You must come and hear her sing this evening. We will be playing at the Oasis Club and we have brought you a ticket."

Mrs. Irani was delighted. She came in good time. I led her to the first row where I could watch her face when I sang. The hall was packed. But I had eyes for only Mrs. Irani. We played for almost two hours. Then I announced that the last two numbers were dedicated to my friend and mentor Mrs. Irani.

The first number was her old favourite, "Somewhere over the rainbow………"

The second was a special number composed for her by Tony.

"You set the songbird free from the prison of my heart

You turned the rain to sunshine on my life

And though oceans now do us part
The perfume of your nearness and love
Will be forever in my heart."

FLIGHT TO FREEDOM

Ammu huddled in a corner of the bus stop, hugging the cloth bag that held all her possessions. She had run away from home and boarded the first bus that arrived in her village. It had brought her to Dharwad. At 5.30 in the morning, it was still dark outside. The conductor plied her with questions.

"Are you travelling alone? Where are your parents? Do you have money to buy a ticket?"

She tried to put on a brave face. "I am going to Dharwad to be with my sick grandmother," she said, handing him the money for her ticket.

The conductor detected anxiety on her face, wondering how her parents could send their young daughter off alone. When the bus approached Dharwad he said, "You wait in the bus stop until it is bright and there are more people on the road."

Now Ammu's bravado had deserted her. She was afraid. "Where can I go? Whom can I approach? My mother will be worried when she finds me missing. Besides, I have taken the money she had kept aside for our weekly provisions." She burst into tears not so much because she had run away from home but because she didn't know whom to beg for help.

"The police? They will take me to the station and probably give me a beating. Or they may send me back home. Will I have to roam the streets till evening? Where will I spend the night?"

Wiping away her tears she stepped out of the bus stop and looked furtively around.

"I have enough money to buy a bun and a cup of tea."

A policeman on the beat spotted her. He was quite experienced in spotting children in distress -missing children, abandoned children or runaway children. He had come across many of them and had rescued them from bus stops, railway stations or while begging on the streets.

"Wait," he said, "don't be afraid. I'm not going to harm you. Come with me to the station. If you're hungry, I'll give you a nice breakfast."

The tone of the policeman was friendly and Ammu felt reassured of his help. He did not ply her with questions. So she followed him to the police station.

"Sit here quietly," he said, "I'll bring you something to eat. Then I'll arrange for someone to come and help you."

The policeman went into the next room and dialed Jahnavi, a child care worker associated with the government-run child welfare organization.

"There is a girl here who looks quite lost. She was loitering near the bus stop this morning. I haven't asked her any questions as I did not want to frighten her. Can you help? The police station is not the best place for her to be."

"Don't let her out of your sight. I'll be there in a little while," Jahnavi said, "And no need to ply her with questions. I'll take over her care."

Jahnavi arrived not very long after. She was a middle-aged lady, soft spoken, with a kind and friendly face. Ammu felt confident that this lady would help her. But there were certain procedures to be followed and Ammu was taken to an institution where several runaway children were housed. She was soon surrounded by a group of noisy, unkempt children, who tugged at her cloth bag and bombarded her with all kinds of questions.

"Where have you come from? You'll have to stay here forever if your parents don't come to take you back."

Ammu began to sob. She backed away from the children and clung to Jahnavi. "Please take me with you. Don't leave me here. I'll be your obedient and faithful servant."

Most of the children were rough and unruly. They had been found begging or stealing or sniffing 'glue' and were picked off the streets. Jahnavi realised that Ammu came from a different background, and it would not be in the child's interest to leave her here.

"Alright, you can stay with me tonight. Tomorrow we'll decide about your future. Now please stop crying and dry your tears."

But when morning came, Ammu began to plead and beg, "Please don't send me away. Let me stay here. I'll be obedient and do whatever work you give me to do. But I also want to go to school. I want to be educated and live a decent life."

Jahnavi had been widowed at an early age. She never remarried. Instead she devoted her life to the service of lost and runaway children. Of late she had begun to feel lonely. Here was an opportunity to look after a young girl. "It will brighten my days caring for her. But before I make a decision, I must know more about the girl's background."

Ammu had not volunteered any information so far. "You'll have to tell me your story if you want my help," Jahnavi said. Between tears and sobs, the girl poured out her story.

Ammu lived with her mother in a village called Savadatti, about 37 kilometers from Dharwad, in South India. Her home was a modest hut in a slum, where many single women lived with their children. Her mother Muthu was still a beautiful woman, even though her hair was peppered with gray. She had once been a devadasi – a temple prostitute, who used to be in great demand.

"My mother now earns her living by belting out songs with a group of old devadasis like herself, in temples around the village. They have melodious voices and have a rich collection of song and dance numbers. Their songs always start with praises to the Goddess Yellamma whom they worship. Then they sing about a wide range of subjects concerning women – about their health, marriage, housework and various problems. My mother has a beautiful voice. She strums on a stringed instrument called '*chowdike*,' another woman keeps time with her brass cymbals, and they make music which the villagers love to listen to. The songs are sometimes soulful, sometimes raunchy, sometimes entertaining. They make a living by this form of begging. They receive alms from devotees, tourists and others. I have learnt many of these songs at my mother's knee. I even learnt some dance movements to go with the songs. But I had no idea what my mother had planned for my future. She allowed me to study in the village school and often talked of the benefits of a good education."

"Then why did you run away?" asked Jahnavi.

"Because she had no intention of setting me free from such a bad demeaning system. I'm just ten years old and she wanted me to follow in her footsteps."

Muthu announced one morning, "We are going to the temple on Yellamma hilltop. I have made a vow to the Goddess and must fulfill it."

"No," Ammu protested, "I don't want to live the life you have led. I want to be educated and live with dignity."

But her mother with the help of several old devadasis dragged her along to the Yellamma temple. It was the night of the full moon towards the end of March. This was a steep climb to the top. There were crowds of women milling around with their daughters, as determined as Ammu's mother, to dedicate their daughters to the Goddess Yellamma. A large group of *hijras* in their colourful attire, added to the commotion, singing, dancing and enjoying themselves.

Ammu wiped her tears and continued, "Even before we reached the temple, I had to go through physical cleansing. There was a large pond supposedly filled with holy water. I was literally pushed into the pond to cleanse me of my sins."

"The water must have been filthy with so many girls in the pond," commented Jahnavi.

"Of course the water was very dirty. There were so many of us jostling for space. To add to our misery and embarrassment, there were hordes of *hijras* dressed up in gaudy attire, with their ugly painted faces, leering at us. They seemed to be enjoying our misery."

Ammu was lifted out of the pond and stripped of her wet clothing. Then she was made to walk naked for about four kilometers to the temple of the Goddess Yellamma.

"I will never forget that night. I was tired, angry and ashamed of my nakedness."

At the temple, Ammu was greeted by one of the temple prostitutes. The girl was given a new set of clothing. A chain of red and white beads was tied around her neck. She was now a devadasi, devoted to the Goddess. She would be a servant of the deity forever, dancing in reverence before the Goddess, keeping the precincts clean, and providing drinking water to the devotees. A sob escaped Ammu's lips.

"Take a break," Jahnavi said, "You can continue your story tomorrow."

"No. I'd rather tell you all and be done with it. The saddest part of being a devadasi was that I could never marry. But I had to be available to give my body to the rich men who visited the temple. The highest bidder would get first preference. But as I had not attained puberty, I could go home with my mother and stay with her until I menstruated. Everyone in our village knew that rich men would buy young devadasis and when tired of them, would sell them to brothels in Bombay, Calcutta and even outside the country. How could my own mother do this to me? I know she has been through such a shameful life. Yet she was forcing me to follow in her footsteps. She could not even tell me who my father was. I think she never liked me."

On returning home after the ceremony, Ammu was determined to run away. She was not going to wait until she attained puberty. She didn't sleep that night. Long before dawn, Ammu crept out of her house with a cloth bag in which she had stuffed two pairs of clothing. The sari which she had been given, and the red and white bead chain were left on a shelf, and the money which her mother had set aside for provisions, went into her bag. "Mother will know why I have run away," she thought, then walked to the bus stand to wait for the first bus to arrive, that would take her away from home.

"That's my story and how I landed at Dharwad," Ammu said, as she buried her face in her hands and wept.

"But as far as I know, this disgraceful Devadasi System was banned many years ago. Rules had been laid down in 1987, for prosecution of parents found guilty of dedicating their girls to Yellamma. They would be punished with imprisonment and a hefty fine," Jahnavi said.

"The custom still functions secretly. Police are bribed heavily to turn a blind eye to this practice. Besides, Police are afraid that by opposing the practice they may be cursed by the Goddess with illness such as leprosy, or white spots on the skin or sterility."

"Will this country never be free of such awful traditions and superstitions?" Jahnavi wondered.

"I'm really glad you escaped, Ammu. I'll do my best to help with your rehabilitation. I'll take care of you until you can look after yourself."

"Thank you Amma. I'll always be grateful. I'm not the first one to run away from the village. Many others have done so before me. That's what gave me the courage to run away. But I don't want anyone here to know that I'm the daughter of a devadasi. I want to start on a clean slate. Let everyone think I'm an orphan."

Getting permission to adopt Ammu was not easy. If the authorities knew that she had a living parent, they would only allow Jahnavi to be a foster mother. The procedure to be followed was a lengthy one and spread over several months. Social workers frequented her house to make sure that Ammu was properly cared for.

"She is only ten years old. You must look after her like your own child. She cannot be treated like a domestic servant," warned one of the social workers, "We'll keep checking on her periodically. Besides, you are a middle aged woman. Do you think you can cope with caring for a young girl?"

Jahnavi agreed to all their terms and conditions. "I will bring her up as my own daughter. Caring for her will be my mission."

Ammu's background was a secret between both of them. A new identity would give her respectability.

"It's better for you to have a new name. By what name would you like to be called?"

"Sitara," Ammu said, "I want to twinkle like a bright star. Someday when I'm grown up, I want to brighten the lives of unfortunate children."

Sitara was admitted to a local school. Because of her village school background, she initially found it difficult to cope with her studies. But she prodded on diligently, helped and encouraged by Jahnavi.

There were many times during the first year when Sitara was troubled by her past – moments of anxiety, fear and doubt about her self-worth. Also lurking in her mind was the guilt of abandoning her mother.

"Does she miss me? Is she angry with me for running away? Should I go back to the village and tell her I am well and happy in the home of this kind lady? But if I dare to go back I may be trapped and punished for being a runaway devadasi."

Jahnavi was aware of the girl's troubled thoughts. She realised that Sitara needed counseling. One could not expect her to easily adjust to a life so different from what she was used to. There were good counselors attached to the Child Welfare Organization where she worked.

"I'll discuss with my boss and she will assign a counselor for Sitara."

Over the next few months, Jahnavi was pleased to see the change in Sitara. There was instant rapport between the girl and the counselor. She was an experienced person who could recognize the vulnerability of this young girl. She encouraged Sitara to express the emotions that were bothering her. Gradually Sitara learnt to perceive things in a different light. The feelings of guilt were replaced by a new self-confidence. She was ready to make the best of her new life.

Simultaneously things changed for the better at school. Being an intelligent girl, she made good progress with her studies. Her shyness was replaced by a feisty confidence. The years passed quickly and Jahnavi was happy that Sitara had blossomed into a happy teenager.

In Savadatti, Muthu was at first upset and angry that Ammu had run away from home. The other devadasis made her miserable by predicting that the Goddess would rain curses on her. She lived in sheer fright for the next few months anticipating all kinds of calamities. But when nothing happened, she was relieved. Now Muthu was even glad that Ammu had escaped.

"I was only fulfilling a vow I made to the Goddess when Ammu had fallen ill as a child. I was afraid of losing her, and in desperation, promised to make her a devadasi if she survived."

Now that matters had been taken out of her hands, she was relieved. Ammu was not the first girl to run away from the village. They had all been rescued either by the Social Child Welfare Department or other organizations that took care of runaway children. They were either sent to school or trained in some skill, so that they could eventually support themselves. None of them had come back to the village. Muthu prayed that Ammu too had been rescued by some such organization.

"Yet I miss her very much. I am getting on in years and not in the best of health. I cannot sing in the temples as I used to. Young women have taken the place of most of the older generation. Earnings have fallen and I can barely keep body and soul together. But I pray daily that I'll be able to see Ammu once before I die."

Sitara was now in the final year at school. She had done well academically and took part in school debates and other curricular activities. Jahnavi wanted her to study further, but wondered how she could afford the college fees.

To celebrate the International Women's Day, the Department of Education was holding a statewide Elocution Competition. It was sponsored by one of the Media Houses. The topic for the competition was "Improving the Female Child's Social Image." The participants would only be from the 12th standard. Sitara was selected to represent her school. She was excited but also nervous. She spent many hours consulting her teachers, reading articles on the subject, and preparing her speech. Jahnavi was as nervous as any parent could be. She prayed that Sitara would not get cold feet while on stage. But her fears were unfounded. For a girl of her age, Sitara made a very impressive presentation. She talked of the low status of girls in rural areas and stressed that only education could empower them. Then she spoke of superstitions and useless traditional practices that ruined the lives of young girls. The Devadasi System prevalent in several South Indian states was a regressive practice where young innocent girls were dedicated to the service of a naked Goddess, which was another name for temple prostitution.

"They are all from the lower castes." she said. "Though there is a law prohibiting this practice, it is never properly enforced. Police turn a blind eye or become partners to this social conspiracy which exploits young lives. How can they ever hope for social change? It is the attitude of society that must first change before one can bring about a change in the lives of such girls. They must be set free from this life of indignity. Only education can expand their horizons, liberate them and make them worthy citizens of our country."

The audience was surprised at the eloquence and authority with which Sitara spoke. There was pin drop silence for a few minutes and Sitara thought all was lost. But then they rose up *en masse* and broke out into continuous clapping. She easily won the competition. The chief guest commented on the maturity of thought in such a young girl. Her pictures were splashed across many newspapers. Media persons jostled with each other to get a few sound bytes from her. The crowning moment came when the Media House which sponsored the competition announced that they would support her further education.

"That has taken a load off my mind," thought Jahnavi. "Now Sitara can choose what and where she wants to study in future."

Muthu had come to the grocery store to buy some jaggery for her coffee. When the grocer tore out a sheet from a bundle of newspapers, to wrap up her purchase, Muthu's eyes fell on the pictures in the papers.

"Wait," she said, holding on to his forearm, "Just let me have a good look at the picture."

"Oh! That's the picture of some young girl who has won a competition. Everybody is praising her speech about Yellamma's devadasis.

Muthu snatched the paper from him and hurried away. Back in her hut she examined the pictures closely.

"It is my Ammu. How can I forget her face? I'm so glad she's doing so well. How cute she looks in her blue school uniform and two pigtails tied with blue ribbon!"

For a long time, she sat there feasting her eyes on the picture. Then she took the paper to her neighbour's daughter.

"Please read what is written about this girl. What is the name of her school and in which town is it? Tell me all that is written about her."

Muthu didn't sleep that night. "I just want a glimpse of my daughter. I may not live for long but I can die in peace knowing that Ammu is safe and happy."

The final exams were over. The 12th standard students were having a little party in the school courtyard before they went their different ways. Muthu had taken a bus to Dharwad and was able to find her way to her daughter's school. Outside the gate was a large mango tree with overhanging branches. She stood there watching the girls having fun. It took a while for her to spot Ammu.

"She looks so grown up and happy. God bless the people who cared for her."

Muthu stood there for a long while watching her long lost daughter. "Now I can go away in peace."

She moved out of the shadows to make her way home and had covered a few meters. One of the students said, "That woman has been hiding under the trees and watching us. I wonder why? Now she's walking away."

Sitara stared at the receding figure. Though the woman was very thin, her gait looked familiar. She rushed out of the gate and caught up with her. Holding her by the shoulder, she turned her around and looked into her eyes. Then her arms reached out and embraced her mother.

"Amma," she cried and melted into tears as they both clung to each other.

A MEMORY TO TREASURE

Sudha drove down the lane in her yellow and black auto rickshaw with no hope of picking up a passenger on this lonely road. It gave her time to reflect on her life so far. After completing her 12th Standard, there was no way she could enrol in College.

"I'll become an auto rickshaw driver," she thought, "And I'll only ferry female passengers. There are so many complaints of auto drivers misbehaving with women."

She had got her driving licence but finding a job was difficult. Owners of auto rickshaws were hesitant to entrust their vehicles to a woman with no experience. She had registered with the Employment Exchange and had been to several interviews. The owners were businessmen who wanted able drivers to ply anywhere in the city, at any time of the day, even at odd hours.

"Sorry I can't employ you. Too young and inexperienced," one said.

"What? A woman driver? You won't survive in a competitive man's world."

"It's not enough to know how to drive. Do you know how to fix mechanical faults if the auto conks out on the road? No, no, I can't trust my vehicle in your hands."

In the end, her father, a peon in a bank, had taken a loan and bought her an auto rickshaw.

"Pa, don't worry. I'm sure we'll be able to pay back the loan in a year or two."

Sudha had been driving her vehicle for almost a year with no mishaps. To stay on the safe side, she only ferried women passengers. They sought her out, sure that they would not be cheated. She was courteous and respectful and women admired her for her independent nature.

Now she was on her way to the auto rickshaw stand in the city and hoped business would be brisk that day. Sudha was proud of being the only female auto rickshaw driver in an exclusively man's world. It was not an easy life as the men resented her presence among them. They tried to demoralize her with their rude remarks and character assassination. She was aware that their animosity arose from two factors – her gender and her Dalit background.

"Must have a thick skin if I want to survive," she told herself. "I couldn't care less. I'm doing an honest job and enjoying it. They can cry themselves hoarse but will not chase me away."

A car was parked on the side of the lane and the driver stuck out his hand to hail her.

"My car has broken down and it will take a while for the mechanic to get here. I have to be at a meeting at 9.30 a.m. and it's already quarter past nine."

"I'm sorry," Sudha said, "I only take female passengers."

"Can't you make an exception this once? It's important that I am on time for the meeting. I will pay you double the fare."

"Very well," she said, observing his worried face, "Not for the double fare. Let's say this is my good deed for the day. Hop in and tell me where you want to go."

Sudha watched him in the mirror. "Must be a very important meeting," she thought, "the guy seems to be on pins."

He kept calling somebody on his mobile and getting no answer.

"Can't you speed up?" he asked.

"No, I have to stick to speed limits unless you want me to be hauled up by the police. In that case you'll never reach your destination on time."

His destination was the State Assembly building. Even before she could stop properly he jumped out of the auto rickshaw, thrust a wad of notes into her hands and disappeared into the building.

"Wait," Sudha shouted, "you've given me more than my fare."

But the man didn't hear. "I've never met such a generous passenger before. Hope this brings me luck for the rest of the day. This guy is obviously not someone who usually travels by auto rickshaw. So I'll probably never see him again."

A few months later, Anil Rao opened his newspaper to see the picture of a mangled auto rickshaw and the body of a young woman on the ground beside it. The inset showed the picture of a face he recognized.

"This is the same girl who helped me out when I was stranded. I wonder what happened. Was it an accident? Could she be dead?"

He read the news item about her. Sudha was the only female auto rickshaw driver in the city. The male drivers were jealous of her popularity. They tried to irritate her in many ways but she kept her cool and ignored them. Things came to a head when Sudha refused to join the strike that had been called by the Union, to pressurize the Regional Transport Officer to enhance the rate of fares they could charge.

"This is the limit," they decided, "If she wants to be one of us she must comply. If not, we must teach her a lesson she'll never forget."

Returning home one evening, a group of men waylaid her and irreparably damaged her vehicle. Then they dragged her out and beat her black and blue, leaving her bleeding on the ground. Sometime later, a Good Samaritan passing that way had rushed her to the hospital, where timely treatment had saved her life.

"I'm glad the poor girl is alive," Anil thought. "Perhaps I should visit her and see if I can be of any help. The hospital bill will be exorbitant. I could chip in towards her treatment."

He made a note of the hospital where she was being treated. "I'll stop by this evening."

When Anil entered her room, he was shocked to see her head swathed in bandages. Her left arm and leg were in plaster. She was deeply sedated. His heart went out to the girl. Her anxious parents hovered in a corner of the room.

"Be brave," he told them, "this is a good hospital and I'm sure she'll get the best treatment."

A policeman stood in the corridor.

"Have they caught the culprits?" Anil asked.

"Not yet. But my bosses are busy interrogating the suspects. The guys are pretending to be innocent. But the police have ways and means of finding out. As soon as this patient awakes, I am to inform them, so that they can take her statement."

The next day when Anil approached the investigating officer, he was shocked by the man's casual attitude.

"She brought this on herself. She has no business crashing into a man's world. Our investigation will take its own time. She has no relatives who can pull strings. Besides, she is only a Dalit. It beats me why a man in your position should bother about a nobody."

It took all of Anil's willpower not to drive his fist into the man's face.

"With an attitude such as yours, it looks like the crooks are never going to be caught and punished. No wonder that the law and order situation in the city is deteriorating. I'm sure you already know who the culprits are. But your palms must have been generously greased to turn a blind eye to such lawlessness."

"Mind what you're saying Sir. Remember you are talking to a police officer."

Anil pulled out his identity card and thrust it into the man's face. He was a bureaucrat attached to the Ministry of Labour.

"Sorry Sir," said the officer, red in the face.

Anil took to visiting Sudha on his way back from work. On the third day he found her awake though still groggy. There was no look of recognition in her eyes. She mistook him for a doctor.

"My head hurts," she complained, "can't you give me something to make the pain go away?"

"I'm not your doctor. Just your well-wisher. But I'll ring for the nurse to bring you something for your pain."

It took Sudha a week before she could ask, "Who are you? Have we met before?"

"Yes we met, and I'm not surprised that you don't remember me. You did me a favour once. You helped me when my car broke down."

A smile lit up her face. "I remember now. You were the first male passenger to travel in my auto rickshaw. You paid me much more than the double fare. I looked out for you for many days, hoping to return the extra money. But of course we live and move in worlds apart."

Sudha had to remain in hospital for three weeks. The doctors wanted to be sure that there were no complications after the head injury. Anil took to dropping in whenever he was in station. When unable to visit, a bouquet of flowers or a box of chocolates would arrive through a messenger.

"Who is this fellow who keeps visiting you and sending gifts?" questioned her father. "You don't want more complications in your life just now."

"He seems to be some important officer," cautioned her mother. "What does he want with a poor auto rickshaw driver?"

"Mother, I'm proud of being an auto rickshaw driver. I believe in the dignity of labour and I suffer from no inferiority complexes. Besides I'm not going to stay this way forever. I have ambitions for a better life."

"All your bravado has got you nowhere. You're lucky to be alive today. Now don't complicate your life by imagining this man to be your friend. He belongs to another world altogether."

Sudha preferred to remain silent.

"Perhaps I'm reading too much into his visits as Mother suspects. He's just a good guy who wants to cheer up a sick girl."

But thoughts of him kept inadvertently creeping into her mind. Anil's kind face, the way his eyes crinkled when he smiled, the aura of quiet dignity he exuded, were something she liked. On the days that he didn't visit, she felt a hollowness inside.

At the end of three weeks the doctors said she could go home.

"Come back after another three weeks to have your plaster casts removed. But if you have any complaints like headache or blurred vision, come back immediately."

"Look at this," said her father, showing her the hospital bill, "It is a very small amount. I checked with the billing clerk and he said somebody had deposited a sizeable amount as advance. Could this be the largesse of your visitor? He has put us in an embarrassing position. How are we to pay him back?"

Sudha's mother was suspicious. "You are hiding something from us. What is the relationship between you two? I'm warning you this will only lead to heartbreak."

Anil had not visited the hospital for a few days as he was out of station. On his return he found that Sudha had been discharged.

"Not even a note to say she was leaving," he thought. "I guess everything happens for the best. I'll consider my visits errands of mercy and put her out of my mind."

Yet he took pains to persuade a nurse to give him Sudha's address and telephone number which was recorded in her file.

"Might come in handy if I ever need a ride in an auto rickshaw."

But it was not easy to put Sudha out of his mind. There was something very attractive about the girl. She had such striking features in a dusky face. Her eyes were like dancing lights when she smiled and her voice was low and modulated.

"A pity that they had to cut off her hair because of her head injuries. By now she must be free of her plaster casts. Let's hope the accident has not left her with any residual deformities. That would be a tragedy. If she's going to drive an auto rickshaw, she'll need all her limbs intact."

Many times, Anil looked at her address and wondered if he could drop in for a visit.

"I'm acting like a smitten teenager," he thought. "Even if she did care for me, it would enrage my parents if I dared to cross class boundaries."

His parents had already started looking out for suitable brides for their son. Though they were not ultraconservative, they still believed that an arranged marriage to a girl from a good family had chances of surviving in a world where the institution of marriage had become a casualty. But Anil showed no interest in any of the proposals that came his way.

"Leave me alone," he told his mother, "when the time comes, my bride will be a girl of my choice."

"So long as you pick someone from our own community and our social standing," his mother said, "Don't forget we have a standard to maintain."

"And you must not forget that this country is trying to do away with discrimination due to caste and creed."

"Oh! That's all political talk. It is revived before every general election. It will take a few generations before caste is abolished, that is if it ever does."

With the change of government in the State, Anil was transferred out as the Collector of a small town. It was a lonely life and his thoughts often turned to Sudha.

"I wonder if she's driving her auto rickshaw again. I hope she won't run into more trouble. Does she even think of me sometimes?"

Sudha was back on her feet, but there was no question of going back to auto rickshaw driving. In the first place, she couldn't afford to buy another vehicle. The Insurance money she received was just enough to repay the loan from the bank.

"You'll have to think of something else to do," her father said, "You can't risk your life again. The guys who attacked you have not yet been caught and punished. Perhaps they never will be. We have neither the influence nor the means to pursue the case."

"Pa, I'm going to study. I would like to go to college and study for a degree in Law. There are many scholarships for our backward communities. I'm eligible for one of them."

Sudha often thought of the Good Samaritan who had visited her in hospital, and even advanced money towards her hospital bill.

"I never got a chance to thank him. I wonder why he went out of his way to help me. All I did was get him to his meeting on time. He had introduced himself as someone attached to the Ministry of Labour. Why did such an important person go out of his way to show concern? Was it just pity? I just hope I'll bump into him some day."

After her graduation in Law which took all of three years, Sudha was lucky to get an internship with the State Human Rights Commission. It was an interesting job. She had to look through many petitions filed by victims where there had been violation of Human Rights and negligence by the police to prevent such violations. It was then that she came face to face with one of her assailants. He had been hauled up by the Commission on charges of domestic violence. As this was his third offence, he was sent to jail. The sight of him brought back the trauma of her accident.

"Sins have a way of catching up," she thought.

The police had not brought any of the men to book, but she was sure that sooner or later, they would be punished like this man.

Anil Rao was back in the city on a new assignment, after just over four years.

"I will try and find out if Sudha still drives her auto rickshaw. I want to make contact with her. But who knows, she might have got married and moved to another town."

He made bold to ask one of his staff if he had ever come across a woman auto rickshaw driver.

"No Sir. Ever since that terrible accident a few years ago, there has never been another woman driver."

"What does that girl do now?"

"I can't tell you for sure. But I hear she has moved on in life. Got herself a good education and is probably holding an important government job. Backward communities today enjoy many privileges which push them up speedily on the ladder of success."

A few more discreet enquiries brought him the information he sought. Now he could hold out no longer. He still had her mobile number and would contact her. One day, when Sudha was helping her mother prepare dinner, her phone rang.

"Anil Rao here. It's been a long time. I wonder if you even remember me."

Sudha's hands began to tremble. She could hardly speak for a few seconds.

"Hullo, do I have the right number?"

"Yes Mr. Rao. What a pleasant surprise! I never got to thank you for your magnanimity."

"Then don't you think we should meet? It's never too late to thank me personally. Are you still driving your auto rickshaw?"

She laughed and the tinkle of her voice echoed down the line.

"That was a very long time ago. I never summoned enough courage to go back to the job after that ghastly accident."

They met at the Coffee Day outlet in Indiranagar. After a few moments of awkward silence, they started talking like old friends, anxious to catch up with each other's news. Though not a beauty in the conventional sense, there was something attractive in the way Sudha talked and smiled.

"I must get to know her better," thought Anil.

"No one like him has ever been interested in being my friend. He seems so mature and dependable –a good person to know."

These thoughts raced through Sudha's mind.

They began to meet a couple of times every week. Both were hesitant to read too much into these meetings. The caste and class divide would be difficult to bridge. There were consequences to consider. It would lead to mayhem in a conservative society.

When Anil and Sudha finally summoned enough courage to acknowledge their feelings and decided to tie the knot, there was opposition from both families as expected.

"Have you lost your mind?" her father asked. "It's okay being friends. But marriage to a Brahmin? They'll skin you alive."

Anil's mother was hysterical. "No, no, this will bring nothing but disgrace to the family."

"Mother, I told you a long time ago that when I marry, it will be to a girl of my choice. As long as we love each other and have the same outlook on life, we'll be happy. We want no interference or advice on how to run our lives."

They believed that they had stifled opposition from both families and were married quietly at the Registrar's office. After a brief honeymoon they settled down in their new home, confident that they would be left in peace. But about two months later when Anil was returning home from work, he was waylaid by a pack of goons. He was dragged out of his car and beaten up severely. His head was bludgeoned with a thick piece of wood.

"Honour killing," they shouted, "we backward castes too have our sense of honour. You cannot poach one of our girls."

They left him on the road to die.

Sudha was in a state of shock.

"You are responsible for my son's death," shouted Anil's mother, "Your goons killed my boy. Get out and never show your face to me again."

"Yes, I am to blame," Sudha thought, "I am indirectly responsible for his death."

At her parental home, her worried father advised her to go out of town for some time until the furore died down.

"Go to your uncle's house. You'll be safe there. Anil's family will take revenge on you."

"No, this time I will not run away. I will see that the people who killed my husband are caught and punished. This is not an honour killing. This is revenge and jealousy. The man who staged the attack is our good-for-nothing neighbour, whose advances I have been spurning for months. He swore that if he couldn't have me no one else would. I have enough evidence to nail him."

She showed her father the message she had received on her mobile. The heartless man could not even wait till she had come to terms with her loss. The message said, "I swore that if I couldn't have you, no one else would. I hope you have been adequately punished for insulting me. Now you have the rest of your life to enjoy your widowhood. Even if you offer yourself on a platter, I will not want you anymore."

"My dear child," said her father, "This man seems to be cruel and heartless. Who knows what else he can do to spite you? It's better that you leave town for some time."

"No, Pa. I will not run away this time. Even if it's the last thing I do, I'll see that this murderer and his gang are arrested and punished."

Sudha was confident that with the support from the lawyers who worked with her at the State Human Rights Commission and the evidence she had on her mobile, the guilty would be punished. She had beautiful memories to treasure and no one could steal them from her. She set out confidently to the police station to lodge her complaint.

LEGALLY UNBOUND

Linda stubbed out her cigarette and moved to the podium where Ronnie was tuning his guitar and Jerry was trying out the drums. They were a threesome who loved entertaining the members of their club every Saturday evening. The Meredith Club on Langford Road was an old institution started during the time of the British in India. It had retained its old world charm with its large spacious halls and high roof, its chandeliers that cast mellow shadows across the rooms, creating a laid-back ambience for an evening of fun and friendship. The membership was expensive and limited.

The musicians were not professionals – just club members who loved music and singing. As many of the members were middle aged, they preferred old numbers – R&B, country music and good old love songs with their soul-stirring lyrics. Not for them the loud cacophonies of the new age that passed as music. After a hectic work schedule during the week, they loved to relax on a Saturday evening – a time to unwind, to make small talk over drinks, to socialize. Music by the trio provided the right mood for such an evening.

Ronnie a surgeon, began a rendition of "What a wonderful you" in a super imitation of Louis Armstrong. Then Linda followed with "Strangers in the night," in her low sensuous voice. Everyone stopped chattering and listened intently to her song.

A stranger suddenly walked up to the podium and literally snatched the mike out of Linda's hands. She had seen him entering the room and sitting by himself at a corner table. "Was he a new member?" she had wondered.

"I want to introduce myself," he said in a voice that smacked of arrogance. "I'm Larry Rego. I've just moved to the city and hope to be here for a long time. You might wonder how I got admission to this exclusive club. Put it down to good connections and money power. I too am a musician of sorts and if you don't mind, I'd like to liven up this evening with a song. It has an African beat. He took up Ronnie's guitar and began to strum. The rhythm was unsettling, and though his voice was powerful, it was more sound than melody.

"Is this meant to arouse the savage beast in us?" someone asked.

"More like a drunken hooligan on the roll," whispered another.

Linda frowned. "What an exhibitionist! Really a vain creature," she thought, "so puffed up with his own importance."

The man turned to her. "How do you like it?"

"Takes some getting used to," she mumbled.

"I'm here for a long stay. So you better get used to my style," he said.

Larry Rego was at the club every Saturday evening. For him Linda was the main attraction.

"I feel like a teenager," he thought, "I can't get the girl out of my mind."

She was everything he envisaged in a lover – tall, slim with sparkling eyes and easy camaraderie with other club members. But it was her voice that set his heart on a gallop.

"She is careful to keep her distance from me. Why did I have to behave like a pompous ass on my very first visit to the club? If I thought I could impress her I was very wrong. It only backfired. But what Larry wants Larry gets. Somehow I must win her over."

As weeks passed Linda did become conscious of Larry's presence. He was knowledgeable and witty and soon won over members of the club. Though Ronnie and Jerry invited him to sing again, he gently declined.

"No, no, you are doing a fine job. I'm glad to listen."

Linda was a painter well known in the Artists' Circle. Though young, she had already caught the attention of critics who predicted a great future for her. Her paintings sold for good prices. Her studio was a spacious garret on the top floor of a bungalow owned by an Anglo-Indian lady. Here Linda could work for long hours without interruption.

She loved the privacy of her studio. She didn't like anyone to see her paintings before they were completed. Besides, she liked the security. Whenever Linda wanted a break, Mrs. Hodges was ready for a chin-wag over a cup of coffee.

Now Linda heard her arguing with some stranger.

"No, you just can't barge into her studio," she said, her voice raised to a high pitch. "She does not like to be disturbed when she's working."

"She'll be pleased to see me," he said confidently and pushed past her.

Linda cocked an eyebrow.

"What brings you here and how did you find this place? This isn't on any tourist itinerary."

He laughed. "Aren't you pleased to see me? I took all the trouble to find the place. I wanted to creep in and observe you at work."

She looked down at her painted stained pinafore and fingers smeared in red and yellow.

"Not a pretty sight," she said.

"Pretty enough for me."

He studied the paintings on the walls. "Hmm. Quite an artist! Are any of these for sale?"

"I'm getting ready for an exhibition. Oh no, you can't have that. It's the best I have," she protested, as he took down a painting of waves pounding a giant black rock, then disintegrating into frothing nothingness.

"This excites me. The immovable strength of the rock and the futility of waves beating against it! I must have it. It reminds me of myself. I'm as solid as a rock. Nothing can move me if I want to do something."

"Wait till the exhibition is over. Then I'll give it to you."

She didn't like the way he ignored her objections.

"Here," he said, handing her a cheque, "I think it's pretty generous for a small painting."

The exhibition was held at a gallery on Lavelle Road. Linda was sharing space with another artist as she didn't have too many pieces to display. There was rich warmth in her paintings. The interplay of light patterns and colour showed that she had achieved a certain degree of technical mastery. The Art World had recognized her as a very promising artist.

Larry Rego came bouncing into the exhibition hall early in the day.

"What a surprise! I didn't think you're the type of person to be interested in Art," Linda said.

"Not just the art but the artist too," he said with a broad smile.

He scrutinized each picture, commenting now and again on colour and technique.

"Are you an artist then? You criticize as though you know it all."

"I have an eye for beauty. Your paintings are good but……"

"But what?"

"Oh never mind," he said and went off to speak to the gallery owner.

Later, Linda was surprised to learn that Larry had bought all of her six paintings.

"He must be in love with you," the gallery owner said, "And it's quite obvious that he is filthy rich."

Larry gradually insinuated himself into her life. He phoned her several times during the day. He insisted that she go out with him to the movies or for dinner. He showered her with compliments. When he was sure that she had fallen in love with him in a big way, he popped the question, "Linda my sweetheart, will you marry me?"

Though she had some reservations about how he cleverly forced her to do whatever he wanted, she attributed it to his love for her. The marriage announcement drew mixed reactions from her friends. Ronnie the surgeon cautioned her to wait and get to know him better.

"He's a businessman and he knows how to market himself. You've hardly known the guy for six months."

Jerry too was not very enthusiastic.

"All that glitters isn't gold Linda," he said.

But the majority believed that it was a match made in heaven. Larry was everything a woman could wish for – handsome, well mannered, intelligent and rich.

"I'm a lucky woman," Linda thought, "He's crazy about me."

Their marriage was the talk of the town.

"Rich businessman weds city artist," screamed the papers, "The city has not witnessed a wedding on such a grand scale for a very long time."

This was followed by an expensive honeymoon in Scotland. Linda, who had never been out of the country before, was absolutely thrilled.

"The lochs, the castles, the highlands – if only he would let me paint some of the scenery!"

"No darling," he said, "We're on our honeymoon and it's our special time together. I can't spare you even for a minute."

Linda felt loved and wanted and hoped it would last forever.

Larry's apartment was run just as efficiently as his business. Linda wondered if this was all a dream. How had she landed in such a luxurious apartment? How did she find such a wonderful husband?

"God is really good to me," she thought as she lay in his arms that night.

"Tomorrow, I'll have to get back to work," Larry said, "I hope you won't feel too lonely all by yourself. You'll find enough to keep you busy – my well-stocked library, music, the works - all under one roof."

"I want to go back to my studio and do some painting. I have some unfinished pieces to finish."

"Give up the studio," he said, "You have the run of this place. Choose a room where you can paint and indulge yourself. Why must you paint in that dingy old garret?"

"It's not dingy. I love the place."

But at his insistence, she shifted her stuff to a corner room with a large window overlooking a school playground. Somehow, it was not the same. Every evening, when Larry got back from work, he'd step into her den and criticize whatever she had begun to paint.

"I can't paint with people breathing down my neck and passing comments," she grumbled, "I really liked the seclusion of my studio."

"Where did you learn to paint?" he asked one day, "Your colours are too gaudy."

On another day, he would say that the paintings looked too gloomy. Sometimes he sneered and said they were so immature. Even a child could do better.

"I guess my marriage has made me lose my ability to paint," she said one day.

It made him angry.

"That's sheer ungratefulness." His tone of voice was almost threatening.

"Have I done anything to stop you from painting? You've lost it because you're not a Picasso in the first place."

Linda fumed. She had a good mind to tell him that she had graduated from the best School of Arts in Bombay and had been painting for many years. In fact, she had earned a sizeable amount of money and had a neat little amount stashed away in the bank.

"But I'm not going to tell him about it. Who knows what he will do to make me totally dependent on him."

His words hurt. They were so critical and demoralizing that she gave up painting all together.

"May be as he says, I'm no good at all. So why waste my time?"

She began to lose her self-esteem and confidence. She realised that this was leading her on to depression. "I'm a bird in a golden cage. The door is so securely closed that I can't think of flying away."

One day when she was pottering around, she found the six paintings Larry had bought in her exhibition, carelessly dumped in the garage. It broke her heart to see the work of her hands treated like so much garbage. Long hours of labour had gone into these paintings, not to speak of the thrill these creations had given her. It made her very uneasy.

"Who is this man I've married? I know very little about him. All I can say is that he excels in treating me as if I am the dumbest creature living. Everything I do is substandard. Everything I say is stupid. I'm beginning to lose my self-confidence. I don't see my friends because I'm afraid they'll see the change in me. I wish I had listened to Ronnie and Jerry."

That evening, she picked up enough courage to ask about her pictures.

"They didn't go with the ambience of this apartment, darling. In fact, I bought them because I didn't want you to be disappointed at the end of the day. I was sure no one would buy them."

Linda bit her lip to keep from sobbing.

"This man is really a devil in disguise," she thought.

But that evening, he was so loving and attentive to her every need.

"My friend has invited us to dinner at his house. I want people to see how beautiful you are and how lucky I am to have you as my wife."

Linda hated these parties but Larry simply loved them. He made himself the centre of attraction. Men hung on to his every word and women simply drooled.

"What a lucky woman you are, Linda! I'd give anything to swap with you even for a night."

She heard one man tell Larry, "You really have good taste in everything. How did you meet her?"

"Love at first sight," he said, "She's my little Eliza Doolittle. Had to work on her some. But she's a fast learner and she's brought so much sunshine into my life."

Linda wanted to puke. How dare he insult her before his friends? Eliza Doolittle indeed!

"Is this man mentally challenged or does he suffer from megalomania?"

Saturday nights at the club didn't happen anymore. There was always somewhere else to go or something else to do. She had lost touch with Ronnie and Jerry and all her friends at the club.

"Why can't we spend Saturday nights at the club? I miss all my friends very much."

"And have you make a fool of yourself? Linda, you're no nightingale. The people who frequent that club are old fuddy-duddies without any clue about good music. Well, you were entertaining them for free. So that was good enough for them. If you want to sing, why don't you sing for me at home? Or in the bathroom if you prefer that?"

"And have you batter me down with insults?"

"You have nothing to complain darling. You are surrounded by the trappings of wealth. You wear designer clothes and expensive jewellery. What's more, you have a loving, doting husband. We are invited to every important social function in town and we dine at the most expensive restaurants."

"Yes, I'm just his arm candy," thought Linda, "I could do without all this if he would only let me be myself without making me feel so useless. The man has a dual personality – a perfect gentleman for society and a sadist at home."

It was her third wedding anniversary. Larry had gone to Delhi for a conference and wouldn't be back for a week. He wanted to take her along but she had feigned illness. She stared at her face in the mirror. It was unrecognizable.

"A face so lifeless, it belongs in a coffin," she thought, "Is this really me? Have I turned into the person he wants me to be – spiritless and good-for-nothing, surviving only in his reflected glory?"

These fits of depression had increased over the last year. Sometimes she felt suicidal.

"The world thinks I'm the happiest person on earth. I'm trapped but I want my freedom. I want to be 'me'."

She had systematically isolated herself from her friends. She felt worthless and incapable of answering all their questions. Living happily ever after was just a myth – a vaporous fantasy. If Larry loved her at all, he had a cruel way of showing it.

But the irony of it was that she had nothing to show – no bruises, no black eye, no broken bones. Only a simmering pain inside that told her she had failed to be a good wife to Larry. He needed someone intelligent, charming, and innovative. She had not lived up to his expectations. Now her episodes of depression were increasing.

"I must do something. I must get help before I start thinking of suicide."

Suddenly she thought of Ronnie, the surgeon who used to sing with her at the club.

He was pleased to hear her voice.

"Linda! What a surprise! Thought you had moved into higher society and forgotten all of us."

"Ronnie, I need help. I'm in deep trouble. Can we meet?"

Ronnie sensed the desperation in her voice.

"I'll be free at lunch time. Will you meet me at the hospital cafeteria?"

Over a meal, Linda poured out her story.

"I don't know whom to turn to. I'm afraid I'll do something drastic – either kill him or kill myself."

"Why have you tolerated this abuse for so long? You should have sought help earlier. Looks like your husband needs more help than you do. He seems to be quite an insecure person in spite of his wealth and achievements. Meanwhile you must climb out of this dungeon in which he has isolated you. Do you have any place to go?"

"I'll go back to my parents in Pune until I feel strong enough to sue for divorce."

"I have a good friend in Pune who is a counselor. I'll talk to him tonight. Be sure you see him. Also keep in touch," Ronnie said, giving her a hug. "Now you be brave."

Her old studio was unoccupied and Mrs. Hodges was pleased to see her.

"Where have you been all this time, my girl? I was hoping you would visit me sometimes."

She listened to Linda's story and felt a surge of pity. "Luckily, no children to worry about," she said.

"No fear of that. He wouldn't want my attention diverted elsewhere."

The happy, carefree, lively girl she knew was now a shadow of her former self.

Linda had to plan quickly. She couldn't afford to wait until Larry got back. Over the next two days, she shifted her personal possessions back to the studio. A sudden brainwave made her retrieve her paintings from the garage where Larry had discarded them.

Leaving all her things with Mrs. Hodges, Linda went home. The counsellor Mr. Kale was an elderly gentleman and Linda felt she could trust him. It took a few months for Linda to restructure her sense of who she truly was. All the pain and humiliation she suffered had to be purged out of her system. In this she was supported by the genuine care and understanding of her counsellor.

Linda also felt the urge to pick up her paint brushes again. The counselor encouraged her to express her emotions through her paintings. The open door of a bird cage with a golden finch in flight symbolized her freedom from abuse. She was now ready to claim her freedom from Larry Rego. Her lawyer though, was not so confident of success.

"Emotional abuse is very difficult to prove. But this is a challenge and I'll do my best."

Surprisingly, Larry didn't put up a fight.

"I won't let you tarnish my image through a long legal battle. I have my prestige to guard. You were never a worthy soulmate anyway. So let it be known that the decision to divorce was mine."

But the tabloids screamed, "Emotional abuse drives city artist away from her millionaire husband Larry Rego."

Now on a Saturday evening, Meredith Club once again resounds with the music of the trio – Ronnie, Jerry and Linda. Linda's voice echoes with a new maturity as she belts out a theme from Hovey's 'Vagabonds,' "Off with the fetters that chafe and restrain......off with the chain."

NO SECOND DEAL

The postman stood at my door, a document in his hands with its ominous implications.

"Registered letter for you Ma'am," he said, shoving a paper at me for my signature.

"Oh my God! You look as pale as a sheet. Have I brought bad news?" he asked, dropping his bundle of letters and staring at my face, as he caught me before I fell to the ground.

When I came to, he was bending over me with concern on his face.

"What happened?" I asked, still in a daze and looking all around me.

"You just fainted, Ma'am."

Then I remembered the document that had triggered such a frightening chiaroscuro of emotions – hate, anger, desolation, grief – at the death of a relationship in which I had invested the best years of my life. The "Decree Absolute" had torn asunder two young people who had once proudly stood on the threshold of life swearing to love each other till 'death do us part.'

It had all happened so quickly. Within a period of six months, my loving, caring husband had drifted away from me into the arms of a young woman whom we both had befriended. She was nothing like the type he would have chosen for a lover. Immature, giggly, and probably just out of school, she had married an older man who could give her the rich lifestyle she hankered after and entry into a social circle that bestowed on her a semblance of respectability.

We often met the couple at Club Concorde where we too were members. We soon became friends. As Olga was so much younger, she often came to me for advice on various matters. Sometimes she visited just for a chat over a cup of coffee. She treated me like an older sister, and it felt good as I had no siblings.

Then tragedy struck. Olga's husband Desmond met with a bad accident. Crushed spinal vertebrae had damaged his spinal cord and paralyzed him below the waist. For months he lay in hospital unable to use his lower limbs. He was miserably depressed and bitter against his fate, wishing to die rather than live a useless life. During those difficult months, we did our best to help Olga, both with her domestic and emotional problems as well as caring for her husband.

After work, Robin my husband, would visit Desmond and try to cheer him up, while Olga took a break and caught up with some rest. When Desmond was brought home in a wheelchair, our care and support for the couple increased. We felt duty bound to help them as best we could. Though I had to give up some of my own activities, Olga needed my help and moral support to cope with her various responsibilities. She was always tired and depressed and wanted encouragement and cheering up. Desmond's illness and treatment had taken a large chunk out of their savings. Olga, who was always poor in budgeting, found it difficult to juggle and stretch their dwindling resources.

I was totally unaware of what transpired between my husband and Olga. Robin had never given me any occasion to doubt his fidelity. He convinced me that he was held up in the office as his workload had increased. Sometimes he said he had to go out of station on duty, which had never happened before in five years of our marriage.

"More responsibility dear," he said when I questioned him, "the higher the position the greater the workload."

So when I was suddenly confronted with the reality that he was leaving me and was filing for divorce, I felt lost and abandoned. It was a pain beyond bereavement.

"Why?" I asked, still unable to fathom the reason for his sudden exit, "In what way have I failed you?"

"Olga needs me more than you do. You're strong enough to manage on your own. Besides, you've got a very good job and numerous friends. But Olga is helpless and needs my support, and I've fallen in love with her."

"But what about her husband?" I asked, surprised.

"Don't you know he is disabled?" he retorted, "He can't be a husband to her. Besides, I think he is past caring."

"Will he give her a divorce too? Who will look after the poor man?"

"We're not shirking responsibility. We'll take care of him till the end."

"Don't you have any morals at all? How can you commit adultery with Desmond in the house?"

First Robin laughed. Then he shouted.

"Don't sermonize."

He had never raised his voice before.

"The world is not filled with prudes like you. Fidelity is out and affairs are in. This is an accepted global phenomenon."

"Go then," I said, "be happy with whomever you wish."

The days that followed were excruciatingly painful. I had been betrayed by the very man I had loved unstintingly. Where had I failed him? Why had he sought solace in the arms of another woman? Such self-deprecatory thoughts weighed me down. Robin had flaunted all forms of decency by moving in with a woman whose husband was an invalid. I felt sorry for Desmond who must have been suffering with similar pain.

Learning to live again on my own was a long and lonely process. Though I had many friends, they either avoided me or tip toed around me, too embarrassed to broach the subject of my desertion or enquire how I was coping.

But I had a steady job that kept me occupied during the day. I threw myself into my work to keep from brooding. I went to the gym three times a week to tire myself out, so I would fall into bed exhausted. But deep inside was this indescribable ache of loneliness and a feeling that I had failed him and sent him seeking satisfaction elsewhere.

"How long will it take to heal?" I wondered.

Then one bright sunny Sunday morning, I decided to take a walk in the park nearby. This was something I used to do every Sunday until tragedy struck. There she was, the dear old lady sitting alone on her bench. I had often stopped to chat with her on my walks.

"Here you are at last dearie." Her voice rang out when I was some distance away. "Where have you been all these months? I thought you had moved away."

Her concern drove me to tears. It didn't bother me that I was pouring my heart out to a casual acquaintance. I told her how my self-esteem had plummeted and my confidence had taken a beating. She placed her hand on mine, and I felt the flow of her warmth and kindness.

"Dear," she said, "Hang on there bravely. Give yourself time to adjust to your single state. Time is a great healer. You're young and good looking. Soon you must develop your own social life. Perhaps a better future awaits you."

It was pep talk that none of my friends had bothered to give me.

"When God closes one door, He always opens another," she assured me.

It didn't happen overnight. But gradually I learnt to let go of the pain in my heart, until it receded into an occasional twinge. If I was to be free of rancour, I had to forgive.

Robin and Olga were still living-in. Their marriage could not be legalized because Desmond was unwilling to sign the divorce papers. A few months later, I heard that he had died in his sleep. Now they were free to marry.

Almost a year and a half went by before I met someone special. He was a Professor of English at a local college, a confirmed bachelor, who had never considered marriage. I liked being in his company. We sometimes met for dinner or a movie or a concert. We had similar tastes in books and music. We were both determined to keep it platonic. I didn't dare commit myself to a permanent relationship and I thought he felt the same. We nurtured our friendship carefully.

Then one day over dinner, Mathew surprised me.

"Have you ever considered marrying again, Valerie?"

"Not really," I said, "But surely if the right man comes along, I'd give it a thought."

"I've been a bachelor for so long that I wonder if I'll be any good as a husband."

"Consider this," I said, "Love may be the most desirable commodity in the world, but it involves a total commitment.

No holding back. And don't for once imagine that marriage delivers happiness automatically. It is something that must be learned and practised on a daily basis."

We left it at that with no promises given or received. Mathew did not call for a few days, and I thought he was put off by my mini-sermon on marriage.

Then something so surprising happened that completely flummoxed me. I was just getting ready for dinner when Robin knocked on my door. I could hardly recognize him. He looked haggard and had aged considerably. I stifled the desire to throw my arms around him.

"What brings you here, Robin?"

He didn't answer for a few minutes, then burst into tears, sobbing so convulsively that he began to gasp for breath.

"Take hold of yourself Robin," I said.

My heart ached for this sad man who had been such a jovial person. What I felt was a deep pity.

"I'm sorry Valerie," he begged, "I know I've put you through a lot of pain. I am reaping the consequences of my wickedness."

His story was something like a horror movie. It was Desmond who had suggested that Olga start an affair with Robin. They were in a desperate financial situation and had reached their bottom dollar. Creditors were baying for their blood. The bank wanted to seize their assets. They were looking out for somebody who could bail them out of their predicament. Robin had walked right into that web of deceit which they had cleverly woven for him.

"I never suspected even for a moment that Olga's profession of love was all a ruse to make me pay their bills. She played her part so well, showering me with her affection, doting on me and making me feel that I was the most important person in her life. It felt so good to be loved by such a beautiful young girl."

"But you are married to her, aren't you?"

"No. I found out in time that she was cuckolding me and was in another clandestine relationship with a very rich man. But what really sent shivers down my spine was her casual admission that she had poisoned Desmond and got him out of the way."

"Oh my God! Did she kill him?"

"Poisoned would be a better word. He died in his sleep after his nightcap was spiked with poison. I became paranoid after that especially when I discovered that she was cultivating a new interest."

All I could feel for the poor sucker was pity. He had walked out on our beautiful marriage, all for nothing. I couldn't even bring myself to say that I was sorry for him. If he had come with hopes of reconciliation, he was barking up the wrong tree.

"Our marriage is dead and buried. It can never be resurrected again," I thought.

As though reading my mind he said, "I'm sorry Valerie, for all the trouble and heartache I have put you through. I want to come back and give our marriage a second chance. I promise I'll never be unfaithful to you again."

"No amount of apologizing can change what you have done. To take you back would be to demean myself. I'm sorry that things didn't work out for you. But I can't help."

"Is there someone else in your life then?"

"That's none of your business," I said, showing him the door.

Long after he had gone, I sat there imagining what it would be like to fall in love again – to nestle cheek to cheek with someone warm and tender, someone who would love me unconditionally and passionately. I hoped that someday soon Mathew would come to me and say, "Yes, that's exactly how I feel."

ENTRAPPED

Meena arrived breathless at the bus stop. It was 5 a.m. in the morning and there was not a soul in sight. Her few belongings fitted into the cloth bag she carried. She used it as a pillow and lay down on the vacant bench.

"I don't know where I am and what is to become of me but I'm too tired to think about it just now. I need some rest."

She had travelled over eight miles during the night, sometimes walking, sometimes running, off beaten tracks, through field and forest until she could walk no more. Now, despite her worries, she fell asleep.

"Wake up," a woman said, shaking her by the shoulders. "The first bus will arrive in fifteen minutes. Where do you want to go?"

Meena jumped up with a start, ready to flee.

"Are you going someplace?" the woman Gulabi asked again.

"Nowhere to go," Meena sobbed and burst into a torrent of tears.

"Come to my house," Gulabi said, "You can rest and when you feel better, decide where you want to go."

Clutching her bundle, Meena boarded the bus along with the woman. She was glad that Gulabi didn't bombard her with questions.

They alighted at a place called Saklespur, at the foot of the Western Ghats.

At teatime, they sat across a table. Gulabi's eyes travelled over the girl. She figured that Meena was no more than eighteen. Her dark expressive eyes in a finely chiselled face mirrored anxiety and sadness.

"The girl is in some kind of trouble," Gulabi thought, "She's a fine specimen of a woman and will make an excellent candidate for our Movement."

Meena realised how helpless she was. "If I want any help from this woman, I'll have to tell her my story. She seems very kind-hearted and I'm sure she'll not send me back."

As she related her story, she played with her long black tresses that were neatly plaited and reached down to her knees.

"I lost my husband a few days ago. I was promptly stripped of all my jewellery and good clothes. My in-laws wanted me to shed my blouse and wear the ugly maroon sari like all other widows in my community. More than anything else, they wanted to shave my head bald and send me off to an ashram for destitute widows. I could not return to my natal home as both my parents are dead. In spite of being fairly rich, my in-laws thought I'd be a burden to them. So I ran away and for all you know, they might have sent the police in search of me. Please help me find a job so that I can support myself and also have some security."

"Of course," Gulabi said, "My organization has helped many women like you. Rich or poor, literate or illiterate, it is our job to rehabilitate such people and restore their dignity. Tomorrow I will introduce you to my bosses."

The jeep that arrived next morning took them high up into the Western Ghats. It was a long drive far away from civilization. All around was dense jungle. Meena wondered if she was being taken for a jungle safari. After almost three hours of travel, they arrived at a clearing in the forest. A number of tents were spread out over a large area. Meena was introduced to men and women in grey uniforms.

"Welcome to our camp," said the Camp Commander, "you will find many people like you for company. I can also assure you of your safety and security. Your life will change overnight. You'll have good food to eat, decent clothes to wear and a steady income. But you must be prepared to work very hard and obey all the rules."

"That I will gladly do," promised Meena. Her in-laws would never find her here. But she was beginning to feel disoriented. "Why are so many gun-toting guys around the camp?" she wondered.

Gulabi led her to a large tent.

"You will not be lonely here. There are twenty other girls living in this tent."

But as it was the middle of the day, the place was vacant. Leaning against the circular wall of the tent were duffel bags and sleeping bags. It was more like a military camp.

"Whatever possessions you have must fit into the duffel bag. Your sleeping bag should be rolled up neatly every morning and stacked against the tent wall as the others have done. Whenever work beckons, we move camp. So we travel light. Now here is your uniform – khaki fatigues and boots. Pin up your hair into a tight bun so that it doesn't get in the way. Or else you will have to cut it short," Gulabi said, making Meena wince.

When Meena had changed into her khakis, Gulabi said, "Now come along. The Commander would like to have a chat with you. He will explain the nature of our work. I must leave you with him and return to town."

"No, no." Meena pleaded, "I don't think I'm suitable for this job. Please take me back."

"You are safe here and will be well protected. I'll be back in a few days and if you still want to go away, I'll see what I can do."

The Commander appeared to be a friendly fellow.

"Sit down and make yourself comfortable. I'll explain the nature of our work and you'll realise what an important job we are doing. We fight for the rights of the poor. The government is in cahoots with greedy industrialists who are robbing the wealth of the forests. Rampant deforestation and mining is driving the tribals from their natural habitat. We fight on their behalf so that they can get back their land, have better jobs and improve their standards of living. We have thousands of armed soldiers and other cadres, not to speak of the millions of peasants and tribals who support us. You are now a member of our Revolutionary Force. We call ourselves Naxalites. You'll be trained in guerrilla warfare and how to wield a gun skilfully."

Meena shivered. "I've never seen a gun at close quarters and I've never even killed a rat so far. How will I kill human beings?"

"You'll learn in good time. We have rigorous training programmes."

As Meena lay in her sleeping bag that night between two other members, she could not help but sob her heart out.

"Stop snivelling and get some sleep," said the girl next to her. "The wake-up bell rings at 5 a.m."

The girl on the other side said, "Whoever comes here never returns to her family. If you try to escape, you'll be shot. So just grin and bear it. We too were lured into this situation."

It was a traumatic initiation into the life of a revolutionary. Someone shook her awake when the bell rang.

"Get up fast. We have very little time to get ready."

The sleeping bags were quickly rolled up and pushed against the tent wall. The morning ablutions were rushed through. Then followed an hour of drill and exercises.

After a frugal breakfast she was marched off to the firing range. A gun was thrust into her hands.

"Hold it and feel the thrill of cold metal."

Meena was terrified and began to tremble. The gun merely sent her into hysterics. A solid slap from her instructor brought on a gush of tears.

"Stop this nonsense. I'm teaching you to be a good soldier not a coward. Now listen while I describe the functions of each part of the gun."

So Meena began her training into jungle warfare. "From the frying pan into the fire," she thought, "I would have probably been safer in the ashram for destitute widows."

After lunch there were dreary lectures to sit through. Most of what was said went above her head. The word 'Revolution' cropped up frequently. This was the *mantra* that was used to brainwash new recruits and keep up the spirits of those already initiated.

"We are fighting against government officials, politicians, greedy landlords and corrupt policemen who have robbed poor people of their property and rights. Aggression is how we will defeat such forces."

These long and monotonous lectures made Meena's head ache. She wished Gulabi would come and take her away from the camp. But Gulabi arrived with upsetting news.

"As you feared, your in-laws have complained to the police about your disappearance. What's more, they say you might have been instrumental in the death of your husband. You'll be safe here. No one dare enter this camp."

All Meena could do was give vent to her tears.

"It's a cooked up story to keep you here. Gulabi is known for spinning such imaginary tales," said one of her mates. "You can never escape from here. There are guards watching us day and night."

But gradually, the brainwashing took effect. She was young and pliable like putty in the hands of the bosses. There came a day when she could handle a gun with ease. She was soon carried away by the momentum of the revolution. She forgot life beyond the jungle. The daily routine of making the Red Salute and swearing allegiance to the cause brought about a steady change.

"I'm beginning to like the thrill of combat. I don't feel queasy anymore when witnessing or perpetrating atrocities on people who are enemies of the poor. These are the very forces who are keeping tribals hungry and powerless. I'm a revolutionary now and should have no qualms about what I do. The aim is to annihilate class enemies."

Looting, robbing, killing became a way of life. Many times they were killing innocent people, the very people they were supposed to protect. The power of the gun was intoxicating. Meena was not only a good shot but an expert at laying Indigenous Explosive Devices (IEDs) to trap police who were always on the lookout for Naxalites. It was so thrilling to see groups of policemen or villagers blown up by these land mines.

Meena became bolder with each passing day. She went into remote villages to recruit women for the movement.

"We are fighting on your behalf so that you can own land, have jobs and improve your standard of living."

All this talk took place while making off with the little food the villagers had and threatening them with death if they squealed to the police. The red corridor controlled by the Naxalites ran through twenty states. They moved frequently along this corridor whenever threatened by the police.

Four years sped by with incredible speed. Disillusionment had already begun to set in. The horrific crimes she committed with such chilling ruthlessness, made her worried that she was losing her humanity. Besides, for all her expertise in armed insurgencies, patriarchal dominance was obvious. Women soldiers were at the mercy of the men.

Meena had blossomed into a beautiful woman. Though they were all sworn to celibacy, she noticed many of the senior officers giving her the glad eye. She had heard whispers from her comrades that girls were dragged out of their beds at night to service the higher cadres. Some never came back. Those who resisted were raped and shot.

"Oh my God!" Meena thought, "My turn may come any time. How am I going to protect myself?"

Meena was on guard duty at her tent one night. She felt a firm grip on her shoulder and one hand closed over her mouth. She was dragged into the interior of the jungle.

"God give me strength," she prayed silently, "I don't want to be mauled by this animal."

The man pushed her to the ground and knelt astride. But even before he could disrobe her, she pulled out the knife she had in her trouser pocket and plunged it into his heart. The rapist was a senior Naxalite officer. Meena didn't wait to see if he was dead. She bolted through the jungle and did not stop till daylight. By morning she was dead tired and couldn't run anymore.

"I will not run anymore," she decided, "I will turn myself in at the closest police station."

She reached a village that was just stirring to life. The lone constable at this police station felt his legs tremble at the sight of this dishevelled apparition.

"I surrender. I'm a Naxalite," she told the man, "But first, can you give me a glass of water?"

Even before he could return, she had passed out on a bench through sheer fatigue.

Senior officials soon arrived and took her into custody. Interrogation was spread over several days until she had given them every bit of information about the Naxalites in the Western Ghats, the location of their camps and the workshops where their pipe guns and bombs were made. Then followed many sessions with the psychiatrist before she could return to normal life. The indoctrination of the Naxal ideology had to be knocked out of her mind. The memory of her harrowing experiences had to be sanitized and feelings of guilt washed away.

"I will not run away again," she decided. "I will stand up and fight for my rights. My in-laws will have to give me a portion of my husband's assets. I'm going to join the Police Force and the money I get will cover my training in Law Enforcement. I will hunt down the very people who entrapped me and thousands of other innocent girls."

LOVE'S MIRACLE

October slipped away in a flurry of activity, and the cold November wind brought with it a nip in the air. While part of me rejoiced for our daughter, a twinge of fear lurked in the corner of my heart.

"Will she be happy?" I wondered, "will marriage bring her true fulfilment as a woman?"

Rathi had returned from the States a few months ago, not just with a new degree in Creative Writing, but with news that she had fallen madly in love with an American boy.

"Dad, he's gorgeous! We've been good friends right through the course and he popped the question soon after we graduated."

"I'm truly happy for you my girl. But how well do you know each other? Does he know all about you? Marriage must not be taken lightly. There should be no secrets between you."

"There are none Dad. I can assure you that Danny knows everything about me and he's willing to make an unconditional commitment to me. You'll see what a great guy he is when you meet him."

Rathi was our only daughter and we wanted the best for her. The normal parental urge to give her a lavish wedding had us in a tail spin. But she was quick to veto our plans. She insisted on a registered marriage.

"This will be the legal tie that binds. It is the only thing that matters. No walking around the fire knotted to a man's dhoti and trailing behind like a piece of baggage. Most girls of my age are living in with partners and are quite happy."

"Then we must thank our lucky stars that you want to be legally wedded. We must have brought you up right."

She had given me a hug.

"Trust me. I'd never do anything to hurt you."

Of course there were the usual rumblings in our family circles.

"This comes of sending girls to study abroad before marriage. They become bold and brazen and want to ape the West in every way."

The registration had taken place that morning. Danny and Rathi exchanged garlands and fed each other with *pedas* in the presence of the Registrar. Then they signed the marriage register, which was endorsed by two witnesses. It was all over in fifteen minutes. They both looked deliriously happy and went off for a drive in an auto rickshaw, as Danny was fascinated by this contraption.

My wife Sita began to sob as she held on to my arm.

"A lifetime to bring her up and then within a few minutes, we hand her over to a stranger. I feel very scared. Will he make her happy, I wonder. She'll be so far away from home that we won't even know if things go wrong."

I could feel a lump in my throat. I too was both sad and worried. Rathi was the apple of our eyes. We had showered all our love on her. She had filled the cup of our loneliness with her very presence. Now she would leave us and cleave to her husband. But I didn't want Sita to know that I too was worried.

"Children are given to us only for a little while. Then they must fly the nest and we parents have to let go," I consoled her. "Now we must rush home and get ready for the party this evening. At least she hasn't objected to that."

Our lawn had been turned into a fairyland of twinkling lights. The caterers were busy laying out the tables. There were single red roses in long stemmed vases on every table. The arrangements seemed perfect. I went indoors to change and I heard Sita and Rathi squabbling over the bridal finery.

"You'll do as I say this once," Sita said, "I want you to look like an unforgettable dream tonight."

"But Mum, this sari is far too gorgeous already. Decking up in all this jewellery would make me look like a Christmas tree."

"Darling, will you listen to your mother one last time? I want no more arguments."

When Rathi came down for the reception, there were exclamations of admiration from all the guests.

"Gorgeous!" they said, "She looks like a princess."

Danny too did us proud. He was dressed in an off-white *sherwani*, delicately embroidered around the neck.

"A lovely couple!" I heard people say, as they pelted them with confetti and wished them a wonderful life together.

I felt pretty emotional that evening. My eyes inadvertently filled with tears. As the guests tucked into the sumptuous feast laid out, I quietly disappeared into my sequestered nook in another part of the garden. I couldn't help but think back to that evening twelve years ago.

My car had broken down and I was forced to take the local suburban train at Churchgate. It was the evening rush hour and the trains were jam packed with people even precariously hanging out of the doorways. I managed to squeeze myself into a compartment. But it was just as difficult to get out at Bandra, with all that pushing and shoving.

The commotion on the platform drew my attention.

"What's happening here?" I asked no one in particular.

A young girl was lying on the platform groaning with pain. No one bothered to help her.

"What happened?"

"She was pushed out of the train."

"Why?"

"She probably got into the wrong compartment," somebody sniggered.

A policeman stood around unconcerned.

"Aren't you supposed to help the poor girl?" I asked.

"I'm on duty," he retorted and walked away.

I lifted her carefully, but she groaned with every movement. She was a slim little girl who couldn't have been more than sixteen years old. I admitted her to the Municipal hospital at Bandra. She said she had no relations in the city. So I gave the hospital my address and telephone number, which they could use in an emergency.

The following day, I took Sita along for a visit.

"Are you in pain?" Sita asked.

"Yes. I have a bump on my head and my back hurts very badly."

"Where do your parents live?"

"They are no more. I came to the city to find a job."

"Why did they push you out of the train?" I asked. "Did you try to pick someone's pocket?"

"Oh no. The compartment was overcrowded and I was standing in the doorway. I got pushed out when people alighted in a hurry."

We were already in our forties and we both lamented the fact that we never had any children. Here was a homeless girl who could do with some help. Being stranded alone in a city like Mumbai was no fun.

"Until you are better and can find something to do, you can stay with us," invited Sita. "We have plenty of room in our house."

And so Rathi came to stay with us. It wouldn't be wrong to say that we fell in love with her. She was just sixteen, with a smooth lovely complexion and a becoming smile. She was shy and didn't have much to say. In fact, she liked to be left alone.

Sita and I talked it over for several days.

"Why don't we adopt her?" she asked, "Rathi could be the daughter we never had."

We broached the subject to her at dinner the next night and her unexpected response threw us into a dither. She burst into tears, her sobs convulsing her slight frame.

"You won't want me anywhere in your sight if you know the truth...... I am a hoax. Even my parents disowned me. Later, unable to bear the shame, they committed suicide."

"Calm down," I said, "Tell us what's bothering you ......Did somebody really push you out of the train or were you trying to kill yourself?"

For answer, she turned her sad eyes at me imploring for compassion. Sita got up and threw an arm around her shoulders.

"Tell us what's hurting you..."

"I'm not a girl," she blurted, "I'm a girl trapped in a boy's body. In a little while my voice will begin to crack and I'll start getting hair on my upper lip. Then I won't be able to pretend anymore."

The silence in the room was profound. Neither of us could speak. It was like a clap of thunder hitting us. We had never suspected anything like this. I remembered the dancers I had seen in the Philippines and Indonesia. One could never tell they were anything but girls. We were right in the middle of a dilemma.

"When do you want me to leave?" she asked after a while, tears streaming down her cheeks.

"Stay with us and be our daughter. We will see how we can help you find your gender identity," Sita assured her.

I was glad that she decided in the girl's favour.

Rathi had already studied up till high school though she hadn't taken her final exam. Sita encouraged her to pursue her studies privately. Distance Education proved a real boon to Rathi.

Meanwhile, I heard of a famous andrologist in Hyderabad and took Rathi to him. He was a man with a heart of gold – somebody who empathized truly with his patient.

"I'm glad you have brought her to me," he said, "Now let's make it our combined responsibility to see that she has a healthy body and a mind at ease."

The programme he outlined was long drawn out. It would take prolonged psychological counselling for gender alignment. There would be a regime of cross gender hormone therapy. Finally, she would have to undergo surgery for breast implants and construction of an artificial vagina. Electrolysis of facial and body hair would also be needed.

Sita and I spent sleepless nights weighing the pros and cons and counting the costs. It would run into many lakhs.

"We'll become paupers," Sita said, "But I think Rathi came to us by Heaven's decree. This will be the genuine test of our love for her."

So we scrimped and saved and cut down on our personal expenditure. It took five whole years for the doctor to pronounce Rathi a woman.

"I feel confident to face the world now," Rathi said, "I would like to go to a proper College."

We could only marvel at her robust spirit. We gave her the support she needed, but without her high resolve, the transformation could never have happened. She was very comfortable in her identity.

After graduation, she came home one day waving a paper.

"Listen my dears, I've got a full scholarship to go to the States for further studies. Someday I'm going to be a writer. I want to make you proud of me."

And now she had not only completed her course but returned with a soul mate.

I was shaken out of my reverie by her voice.

"Dad, what are you doing here sitting all by yourself? The guests are leaving."

She embraced me. "Be happy for me," she begged, "This is my finest hour."

As Danny and Rathi went off on their honeymoon, Sita and I clung to each other.

Our large house was up for sale to tide over our accumulated debts. We would soon be moving into smaller quarters. We had no regrets. The words of Booker T. Washington echoed in my ears like a sweet benediction.

"The one thing worth living for and dying for is the privilege of making someone more happy and more useful."

"Yes dear," Sita said, "We may have emptied our pockets. But thank God we never economized on love."

HER TREASURED SECRET

Ritu slumped in her armchair, resting her weary legs on a foot stool. In her hand was a tall glass of Bacardi Coke, and she sipped on it savouring the ice cold drink as it trickled down her parched throat.

"How nice it is just to relax and enjoy my own company!" she thought. "I should seriously think of retiring. Now that I've achieved all that I set out to do I can afford to call it a day."

With the help of her maid she had put away most of her precious possessions. Her clothes were neatly stacked in cupboards, with moth balls generously scattered on every shelf. The house looked almost bare except for the few pictures on the walls. She was no connoisseur of Art, but someone had mentioned that they were a good investment. Paintings of Goddesses exuding sensuality, reproductions of titillating carvings of Belur and Halebid adorned the walls. Anyone entering her house could tell at a glance what her profession was.

"I'm finally on holiday – the very first one in my life. Don't know for how long, but there's no hurry to get back."

Ritu's excitement was tinged with nervousness too. Though she had travelled to a few places in India on her assignments, going abroad was something new. She hoped she wouldn't draw attention to herself by committing embarrassing blunders.

"In a way, my life is a success story of sorts. Most people wouldn't condone the route I've taken. But those who criticize may have never experienced the pain and desperation I've been through. I've harmed nobody. Perhaps I've even brought happiness to some lonely lives. They say, " 'God helps those who help themselves' and He has surely helped me."

She had a few hours more before she could head for the airport. Her ticket to Australia and back, her foreign exchange and other documents had been safely tucked into a roomy brown handbag. She knew she would look dapper in her sober brown pant suit and comfortable shoes to match.

"No one will ever suspect who I am," she giggled.

But then, a wave of emotion swept over her and she burst into tears.

"No, I'm really not proud of who I am. Just a cheap hussy capitalizing on Man's lust! And no matter how I look, I'll have to carry that shame to my grave."

Ritu was married at seventeen, even before she could pass her matriculation. Narayan was a teacher in a government school and they made a pretty couple.

"Such a caring, loving husband! He taught me what marriage was all about. My Narayan was tender in his love making and always put my needs before his own. 'We must live together in such a way that we feel secure in each other's love,' he used to say."

With the arrival of their daughter Gita, their happiness was complete.

"A daughter changes the emotional tone of the home," he said, "She is such a beautiful baby."

But two years later, tragedy struck this family. Narayan lost interest in everything around him. He withdrew into himself, excluding Ritu and the baby from his thoughts. He was lethargic most of the time either curling up in bed or staring vacuously into space. He soon lost his job and the little savings that they had was used up. People said he was possessed, and many mantras and pujas followed. There was no psychiatrist anywhere in their district.

Ritu tended him as best she could. But with no money coming in she had to find a way to keep the home fires burning.

"I would beg food from the neighbours, but there was a limit to their generosity. Hunger and desperation drove me to the streets. I would slip out at night when my husband and daughter were asleep and return hours later, with a measly twenty rupees in my hand."

Narayan was growing increasingly insane. He would throw off his clothing and wander naked through the streets, muttering to himself. Urchins pelted him with stones and called him names.

"When the neighbours came to know of my nocturnal activities, they drove us both out of the village."

Ritu had to find help. If she could find somewhere to leave husband and child, she could go looking for a job. Narayan was attracting too much attention. At the next temple they passed, she left him muttering on the steps. There was no one around. She prostrated before the idol inside.

"Swami, let the priest look kindly on my husband and give him shelter."

With Gita on her hips and a small bundle of her possessions on her head, she kept walking until she could walk no further. She came to the edge of a small town.

"I am ready to drop down dead and must find a place of rest. This child too keeps whimpering nonstop. If only I could find some poison for both of us! That's the best way to end it all."

They were both exhausted, and fell asleep on the vacant verandah of a house, the child in the circle of her arms. Sometime later, she woke up to see an old man staring down at her. He was dressed in a clean white shirt and mundu with a white shawl draped over his shoulder. There was a sandalwood paste mark on his forehead and his hair was pulled back into a top knot.

"Don't be afraid my child. I've been watching you from my dispensary opposite. You seem to be in some kind of trouble. Come with me. I live only a few yards away. I am an Ayurvedic Pundit. Come…" he said.

After a hearty meal which the pundit's wife served, Ritu poured out her story

"I feel guilty that I have abandoned my helpless husband. I wonder if the temple priest will give him some food and let him stay."

"Don't worry. Sooner or later someone will take him to an institution for mental patients where he will be cared for. But what are your plans?"

"Ayya, Amma, would you be so kind as to keep my child with you until I find a job and a place to stay?"

The couple readily agreed.

"We live alone and we have no children or grandchildren. You have nothing to fear. She will be well cared for. We will love her as our own."

Thanking them a thousand times, Ritu stepped out of house when Gita was asleep. It was a heartrending moment. But the old couple seemed good people.

She finally found a job washing dishes at a roadside restaurant. It was on the National Highway where truck drivers stopped for a meal and some rest. From washing dishes, she soon graduated to the position of resident prostitute.

"It's only a job," she told herself, "No strings attached."

She was just twenty, and with three square meals in her belly, her body began to fill out in the right places. Ritu earned a tidy sum. She retained a small portion for herself and sent the rest to the pundit and his wife.

"I cannot come personally as my employer will not give me leave," she bluffed.

"Gita is growing up well and is a healthy child," the pundit wrote. "We are looking after her like our own. She has brought sunshine into our old lives. You don't have to worry."

It was five years before Ritu summoned the courage to visit her daughter. She was sure that the pundit would see through her and despise her for the profession she had chosen. She had learnt the wiles and cunning of her trade. But the richer she grew the more her self- loathing.

The manager of a dance bar in Bombay stopped at the restaurant for a meal one day. He could spot a good bargain when he saw one.

"You're meant for greater things than this roadside dump," he said, "If you know how to wiggle your body, you can join my dance bar."

"But I don't know how to dance. I've only learnt a few movements by watching TV," Ritu said.

"That will do for a start. Go pack your bags while I talk to the Manager."

"I cannot come immediately. There is something I have to do before I leave."

"The sooner you come the better," he said, handing her his card.

Ritu arrived at the pundit's dispensary at noon the next day.

"I am going away to Bombay for a better job. Before I go I'd like to see Gita."

"By all means. But will you be able to answer her many questions? Will you have the courage to tell her what occupation you are engaged in? I have told her that you are a clerk in a government office. Someday she will have to know the truth."

"Not yet," begged Ritu, "Maybe when she is older. I'm doing this so that I can give her a better future. A good education will take her a long way."

Ritu's heart missed a beat when a school girl in a blue pinafore approached. She was tall for her seven years and looked happy. Her hair was plaited in two strands with ribbons to match her uniform. It took all of Ritu's will power to refrain from throwing her arms around the girl.

"Ajja," she said, embracing the pundit, "You know what happened in school today...? Come let's go home. I want Ajji also to hear."

Ritu quietly slipped away, tears in her eyes.

Bombay was a place of immense possibilities. As work in the dance bar began only in the evenings, Ritu had time to take lessons in dancing. She wanted to perfect her numbers. Her eyes were set on the Film industry, where she knew the pickings would be better.

"When I have earned enough, I will have a decent apartment and then Gita can come to stay with me." This was her dream. "I'll make up for all the years we've spent apart. I'll tell her the story of my life and I hope she'll understand."

Years went by. Gita passed her SSLC with distinction. The pundit and his wife were the only relations she knew. They were her Ajja and Ajji. They rejoiced in all her achievements and encouraged her to study further.

"You must be able to stand on your own feet before we die. A good education will help you find a good job. But even after we die, there is someone who will take care of you. You must meet her soon."

Ritu was excited as she planned a special trip to meet her daughter. She had come loaded with presents for all of them.

"Today I'll introduce myself to her as her mother. If she's willing to come and stay with me, she'll lack nothing."

Gita looked forward to meeting her benefactress. She had been told that they were able to live a comfortable life and also send her to the best of schools only because of the lady's generosity. While Ajji prepared the soft fluffy *vadais*,

Gita ground the chutney on the old grinding stone. There was rich carrot halwa too, and Ajja had plucked a fresh bunch of bananas from their tree.

Ritu arrived from the station in a taxi, and the couple rushed out to greet her. As they settled down to tea, Ritu nervously asked "Where is she?"

Gita had worn her best salwar kameez and had stuck a strand of jasmine in her hair. As she came through the door head bowed, Ritu smiled.

"How much she resembles her father! How proud he would have been if he were sane and still alive!"

"Gita, come and greet this lady," Pundit called, "she is your long-lost mother."

Gita looked up into Ritu's eyes and her face contorted in pain.

"No – No, she cannot be my mother. I've seen her face in the newspapers several times. She is the Item Girl who has been booked for obscenity several times. Oh yes! I've seen her photographs – half clad, immodest, gesturing shamelessly at the men around her. She's a liar. She's not my mother."

It was the cry of an injured animal. She dashed out of the door. Ritu burst into tears.

"She hates me and I can't blame her. My life is nothing to be proud of. I can understand her shock at discovering that her mother is a common whore."

She went out to the waiting taxi, wiping her tears.

"I will never come back again. It was sheer fantasy to expect her to welcome me with open arms. When I abdicated my responsibility as a mother, I took the risk of losing her."

On a rebound, Ritu threw herself into work. Her sensuous performances made her very popular with the crowds. Now she could name her price for each stage show. Though the charges were steep, people were ready to hire her.

Ritu moved into a fashionable neighbourhood. Her apartment was done up by an expensive interior decorator. People who had previously snubbed her now doffed their caps when she drove past in her maroon Innova.

"Money speaks," she thought, "And money brings power. All other shortcomings are condoned or forgotten. Even the bloody policemen who harassed and fleeced me for so many years are now ready to bow and scrape."

But for all her wealth, she had never felt lonelier. All her maternal yearnings craved for the girl who had spurned her like so much garbage. She recalled the loathing in Gita's eyes when she was introduced as her mother. If there was such a thing as a broken heart it had happened then. "Even if hearts do mend," she thought, "the keloids that are left behind are ugly."

The pundit and his wife were both dead, and Ritu lost even that tenuous connection with her daughter. "And so I went on living, pretending not to care but dying a little bit every day. Would I ever see her again? Would she never forgive me?"

Ritu was nearing fifty. Most people would say, "Too old to be an Item girl." But she had preserved her figure through rigorous workouts and diets. She was confident that she could still beat the newcomers.

Even so, in the last one year, the thought of retiring had crossed her mind.

"Why do I have to kill myself by working so hard? When I retire I have enough to live comfortably, thanks to my sound investments. I've come a long way from street prostitute to bar dancer to Item Girl. I've earned my rest."

There had even been a few proposals in her lifetime. Some were good men who wanted to make an honest woman out of her. But the majority were undesirables out to exploit her and feast on her money. She had turned them all down. Deep in her heart she hoped that Gita would return to her one day.

And then last month, a letter had arrived from Australia. Turning the letter over and over, Rita wondered, "From whom can this be? No one ever writes to me – and that too from a foreign country."

She tore it open, searching for the name of the sender.

"Gita! Oh my goodness! Does she want to inflict new wounds by lashing out at me?"

She sat down abruptly as her legs had begun to tremble.

"Mother," she wrote, "it feels strange to call you Mother. I've been so judgmental. Put it down to my naiveté. Before Ajja died, he told me the story of your life. I know the reason why you kept your distance. You wanted to spare me the stigma of being your daughter. Even so, it has taken me a very long time to write this letter to you. I am truly sorry and beg your forgiveness. I will soon be getting a good job and I want to make Australia my home. Would you consider relocating to this country and leaving your past behind? We could still have many happy years together, and I promise to look after you."

After the initial shock it was time for jubilation.

"My daughter has finally called me Mother. I must go at once and meet her. What a wonderful reunion that will be!"

She went about, secretly making her plans to go. No one even knew that she had a daughter. But relocating to Australia – that was a different question. She would first have to see if Gita and she could really hit it off.

Rita was shaken out of her long reverie by the doorbell.

"Who the hell…" she thought, "and that too so late. The guy seems to be leaning on the call bell. What can be so urgent?"

She flung open the door, ready to yell at whoever was there. Light bulbs flashed in her face and all around her, and a news hound tried to push himself in.

"Get out," she said, giving him a shove, "What on earth is all this? Could the news have spread already? Oh these terrible reporters. Always barging into other people's lives. I'll be gone in a few hours. Who cares what they write? I've been in the papers before for all the wrong reasons."

The morning newspapers carried Ritu's photo with the caption:

"ITEM GIRL DREAMS BIG – DAUGHTER A COMPUTER ENGINEER IN AUSTRALIA"

"*Clever sleuth unearths one of the best kept secrets...........*"

RUN WHILE YOU CAN

In Mandira Studios the tension in the air had reached explosive proportions. Shooting had been scheduled for 7 a.m. The Director, crew and other film stars had been waiting for the leading lady Nakshatra, who hadn't arrived even by noon. Time wasted meant money lost.

The junior artists began to grumble.

"Damn her. How can she be so inconsiderate? Doesn't she realise that people like us have to rush between studios for our bit parts?"

"Oh! She couldn't care less. She delights in stretching people's nerves to snapping point. Thinks it's her prerogative to keep the whole studio waiting."

"Must have had a late night *yaar*. She's known to be a party animal, breezing through the foyers of 5-star hotels on the arms of the rich and influential."

"Or perhaps she's recovering from a hangover. They say she drinks like a fish. Why do these rich glamour girls have such self-destructive tendencies?"

Director Darshan was worried. Unlike other actresses, Nakshatra was always on time. She never flaunted her stardom or threw tantrums on the set.

"She's been shooting for four films simultaneously, and she's just a young girl. But she's never defaulted before. I wonder if she's ill. Her mobile has been switched off, and no one is answering her land line."

Darshan felt something was amiss.

"I wonder if it's some marital problem. The man is a leech. Doesn't do a spot of honest work, but lives like a nawab. He's supposed to be managing her finances......I feel he's milking her dry, living it up as he does. Anyway, it's none of my business."

Darshan postponed the shooting to the following day. Nakshatra was his protégé in the film world and he felt a certain proprietorial concern for her. He had directed her in several films, and took some credit for her rapid rise to fame. He first spotted her at a school function – a nubile sprite with a halo of curls that danced over her shoulders when she shook her head. He cast her in his first movie and it had catapulted her to instant fame. It had brought him recognition too.

"Of late, she hasn't been herself. She seems worried and preoccupied. Could be overwork."

Darshan had been sorely disappointed at her choice of a lover. Vinod had appeared from nowhere – a real Casanova with a handsome visage and raw sensuality that proved irresistible to the rich young starlet. Though he was moderately intelligent, he had the craftiness of a fox and knew how to woo a young girl and make her feel special.

"You're too young," Darshan cautioned, "you're still in your teens and have your whole future before you. Don't weigh yourself down with such a worthless relationship."

But there were stars in her eyes.

"He loves me very much and makes me happy. I need someone steady and dependable to whom I can come back after a day of shooting."

But there was a gradual change in their relationship. Darshan could sense that all was not hunky dory as she expected. She threw herself into work in a mad frenzy. As Nakshatra got busy with her tiresome shooting schedules and her films set the coffers ringing, Vinod took on the role of her Finance manager. Her friends disliked the man, Darshan most of all. But he felt Nakshatra would brook no interference.

"My concern is only with her acting," he thought, "I'm no guardian angel. What she does with her personal life is not my responsibility."

Even a fortnight after her disappearance, Vinod had not reported the matter to the police. It was only after Producers and Directors from Bollywood fumed and fretted that they were losing money and hollered for some action to trace her, that Vinod eventually registered a case with the Missing Persons' Bureau. The police did some cursory investigations, and as Vinod showed no great interest in pursuing the matter, they closed the files.

"She's a grown-up, wealthy woman. Perhaps she disappeared of her own volition. We have no leads to follow," the police said.

"Good riddance!" thought Vinod, "Now I can live comfortably for the rest of my life. If I'm lucky she may never come back. She knows about my other peccadilloes. It has broken her heart and her spirit, to think that I've spurned her love when the world is falling at her feet. Emotional abuse is a very powerful tool to demoralize a woman. Put an axe to her vanity and she'll just crumble into dust."

Far away in Darjeeling, a woman stood at her window, gazing out at the distant snowy peaks of the foothills. The rays of the setting sun painted the white peaks in golden orange hues, like honey dribbled over ice cream cones. This was her favourite time of day – the quiet moments when day softly gave way to twilight, when a deep contentment washed over her soul like a timeless melody. Here at these heights she had at last experienced a peace which had eluded her for seven long years.

The ringing of the bell shook her out of her reverie.

"Dinner time," she thought, "Can't afford to keep my charges waiting."

With no qualifications to brag about, she was just glad that this residential school had employed her as a warden. They were always short of staff as not everybody fancied looking after a bunch of village girls.

"This place is so far removed from the civilized world that no one will ever find me here," she thought, "This is where I will learn to live all over again like a normal human being. I want to enjoy the fellowship of these simple, uncomplicated people, to communicate, to empathize, to just be me. I lost my best years to the film industry. I might have gained some, but I've lost much more."

She was seated at the table now, surrounded by girls of different ages and sizes. They came from the poorer villages surrounding Darjeeling. The Principal of the school was a rich philanthropist. His life's vocation was to educate poor Nepali girls, who would otherwise find themselves in the brothels of Calcutta or Bombay.

"You look very young yourself," the Principal had said, "And with no experience of handling a bunch of unruly village girls, I wonder how long you'll survive. More experienced and older women have turned tail and run."

"Try me." She was now Veena Sheshadri, the name by which she had been christened. She had discarded the more glamorous Nakshatra by which she was known in the film world.

"My youth will be an advantage," she said, "I'll be able to relate to their problems and understand their needs and frustrations. Besides, I'm in need of rehabilitation myself."

The Principal looked alarmed. As there was no TV in the school and no movie theatres in this area, he was blissfully unaware of her identity.

"What? Are you in some kind of trouble? I can't take on any more problems than I already have – ungrateful parents, undisciplined children, frequent visits from the Social Welfare sleuths to see if the children are being exploited, and the police who are always prowling around to see where they can pinch a penny. And now you?"

"Look Sir," Veena said, "I'm not in any trouble. I'm neither an absconder nor a vagrant. I have skills like singing and dancing which I can teach the girls. You wouldn't want them to be merely bookworms, do you?"

"Okay, I'll try you out for a month. Remember these girls come from a low social stratum. They can be rude and bothersome. You'll have to enforce discipline and it won't be easy. Besides, I can only give you a small salary. This is a charitable institution."

It didn't take long to find out how tough and frustrating her job could be. They were quite an undisciplined group, and the language they used was simply shocking. In the early days, Veena, who had never prayed before, now cried to God, "Quieten my nerves and slow down the impatient thudding of my heart. I came to these hills lured by the tranquillity here and not to be caught up in such pandemonium."

But gradually as she began to know the girls better, she realised that a change was slowly taking place in them. As their basic needs were met and as they became aware of their own uniqueness, they grew into confident young women.

Though Veena was not involved in their academic progress, she was always ready to help those who lagged behind in their studies.

Now as her eyes skimmed over the group, she felt a sense of achievement.

"This place is more a home to us than our own huts in the village," someone said.

"You're like a young mother with a large brood of children. The previous wardens used to rant and scold us for the slightest mistake. It made us worse than we already were," piped in another girl.

She quite liked getting these compliments from the children. It made her satisfied with the course her life had taken in the last three years.

The after-dinner sessions were what the girls loved best. Veena had a beautiful voice and she taught them many lively songs. They were from some of the films she had acted in. For those who liked to shake a leg, she taught them how to dance. During the long winter months when darkness came early, they would huddle around the blazing fireplace, listening to her stories from another world – a world from which she had fled.

The Principal and his wife were very appreciative of her skills. She was only a chit of a girl. Some of the students were almost her age. Yet she had imbued in them a sense of self-worth that had brought about a remarkable change in their behaviour.

"You are as great as the thoughts you think and the values you live for," Veena told them, "So dream great dreams and plod on till you see them come true."

Yet the Principal sometimes worried about Veena. She had no friends and during these three years, she had received neither a phone call nor a letter from anybody. In her leisure hours, she would get on an old bicycle and pedal off to a pine forest close by, until she came to a gurgling stream. From here, she had a wonderful view of the foothills of the Himalayas.

"I love this place," she would think, "The air is so pure. Except for the gentle breeze blowing through the forest, everything is so silent. I feel at peace with myself – a deep contentment like a soft melody in my soul. And somewhere inside me is a new strength and a conviction that someday I can return to the world I have left behind."

The annual School Day was approaching and the girls were very excited.

"Teach us some nice dances and songs," they pestered her, "Our parents and relatives from our villages will surely come. We want to show them how much we have learnt here."

One little girl said, "My father didn't want to send me here at all. He thought I should be earning a good wage as a maid in some rich lady's house."

"I had to look after my brothers and sisters when my parents went to work," said another, "We never had enough food and were always hungry."

"You don't have to think about the past. You have your whole future before you. So work hard and you'll reap your rewards."

Veena choreographed a simple dance drama which the girls could perform. There were other songs and recitations too. The parents were thrilled to see their children on stage.

"We were so reluctant to send our children here. But look at them now – they've turned into little ladies," they said.

In his speech, the Principal complimented Veena on her work and effort.

"You have performed miracles with these girls," he said.

"They have done as much for me," thought Veena.

But she felt very uncomfortable when the Chief Guest kept staring at her. He looked as if he'd seen a ghost. Veena tried to move out of his sight.

"He makes me uncomfortable," she thought.

After dinner, he moved towards Veena.

"Ma'am, I recognize you – even without your grease paint and jazzy clothes," he said with an air of triumph, "You're Nakshatra, the movie star. You can change your appearance and your costume, but you cannot change some of your mannerisms."

"I'm Veena Sheshadri," she said, looking him in the eye, though her voice felt a bit shaky, "You do have quite a fertile imagination."

"You are supposed to be dead. The papers said that your rotting body was fished out from some creek, two months after you disappeared."

Veena felt a chill run down her spine.

"We don't get the newspapers here nor do we watch TV. So I really don't know what you are talking about." She was very convincing.

"Sorry," he said, "I must be mistaken. But what an uncanny resemblance!"

Darshan was in Gangtok, scouting around for a suitable location for his next movie. Nakshatra's disappearance and the recovery of her body two months later had made him so depressed that he had taken a long holiday from work, unable to blot out memories of her from his mind.

He was dining at a restaurant in Gangtok, when he overheard a conversation at the next table. He pricked up his ears.

"You won't believe this," the man was saying, "last week I was Chief Guest at a school function in Darjeeling. The warden there was a young woman. I thought she was the actress Nakshatra, who died under tragic circumstances. I even made a fool of myself confronting her."

"Man, were you having hallucinations? Didn't they say her rotten body was fished out of Thana Creek?"

"She looked at me as if I was insane. I felt quite stupid and embarrassed."

Darshan was out of the restaurant like a bolt. "Oh God! Let it be Nakshatra," he prayed. He reached Darjeeling at night, but the watchman wouldn't allow him on the premises.

"This is a Girls' Hostel Sir, and the rules are strict. Come back tomorrow."

He cooled his heels at a hotel for the night but sleep was evasive.

"I mustn't get my hopes too high. According to reports, the girl has been dead for three years now. If she is living, someone would have spotted her earlier."

The next day the unsuspecting Veena came down to meet her visitor.

"Must be another parent wanting to take her daughter home," she thought, "The reason is always the same. Either there's no one to care for the siblings or there's a proposal of marriage. It will take a lot of persuasion to convince her to leave her daughter in school."

The shock on her face when she saw Darshan was staggering. She stopped in her tracks unable to negotiate the next few steps.

"Nakshatra..." Darshan rushed to her side. They sat in silence for a while.

"Why?" he asked after a while.

"I escaped only to preserve my sanity. I had nightmares of turning into another Parveen Babi or killing myself with alcohol like Meena Kumari. For seven years I was running from one studio to another doing so many different roles, that I couldn't figure out who I really was. I lived in a world of make-believe. I had lost touch with reality......Just couldn't take anymore."

Darshan didn't commiserate. Something had triggered her flight and sent her scuttling like a frightened rabbit into its burrow. She had not told him all. Finally, he said,

"Have you given thought to the number of Producers who have lost crores on your unfinished films?"

"For them I have no pity at all. They have exploited many an actress and left them in the lurch when their films failed to hit the box office."

"What about your husband? Don't you have a care for him?"

The contempt in her eyes shocked Darshan.

"Husband? He's a venomous rattle snake."

At this she burst into a torrent of tears.

"I was afraid for my life. He's a sadist. Mutilating my body gave him a sexual 'high.' If only you could see how my body is criss-crossed with scars! I endured it all for seven long years of our marriage. But I became suddenly afraid that he would one day attack my face and my limbs. And you know my face was my fortune."

"You could have put in for a divorce. You have friends in the Industry who would have helped."

"He would have never let me go. I was his 'goose that laid the golden eggs.'

"Well, he identified a putrefied body fished out of the Thana Creek as yours. Not only has he inherited all your wealth but he has got himself a new wife. Come and show him you are very much alive, and retrieve what is yours."

"Then its time I returned to base, though I loathe leaving this place. Here I've discovered the joy of living again. It has given me a glorious sense of freedom. I'm never going to return to the glamour world."

Nakshatra checked into a small hotel in Goregaon. It was far removed from the 5-star splendour she had once been used to. Her fans would not look for her here.

When she arrived at the police station the next day, the Inspector clutched at his heart.

"I'm lucky I don't have a weak heart Ma'am. I can swear that we fished you out of the creek two months after you disappeared."

"I'm alive and kicking as you can see, Inspector. I need to take possession of my house."

"And your husband…?"

"He won't be there much longer. But you've got plenty of work to do. You've got to identify the corpse you buried. Someone somewhere must be searching for a lost woman."

"That won't be possible."

The thought of exhuming a decomposed body worried him.

"Don't make a mistake this time Inspector," she said, "Here, take these papers. They might help."

She thrust a bulky envelope into his hand. She had retrieved it from her safe deposit box that morning. It was the letter that eventually triggered her flight. It was from a woman called Nina.

"I am Vinod's third victim," she wrote, "The first two have disappeared without leaving any traces. I was lucky to escape. But I made the mistake of challenging him and threatening to expose him. He says he won't rest until he finds me and silences me forever. I too was rich and famous, and I trusted him implicitly. Don't make the same mistake...... Run while you can......"

Nakshatra knew that it would be a long wait before she was free. The Law worked at snail's pace in this country. She would need to find a good lawyer to hasten matters and put Vinod behind bars. It would be worth the wait.

A TIME TO MEND

They lay side by side on the enormous bed. He was curled up in the foetal position, softly snoring beside her. The marital ritual was over. The last two years had seen them grow apart, each silently brooding over their fears and frustrations, unable to communicate, and reluctant to discuss the widening fracture in their marriage. Romi lay still as a statuette, wrapped in her own dismal thoughts. She was awake for most of the night. Sleep when it did come, was the sleep of exhaustion, neither restful nor refreshing.

"When did I last have a good night's sleep?" she wondered. "It makes me irritable and cranky. People at the office have begun to notice and Jatin doesn't care."

Tears rolled down her cheeks when she thought of the early years of her married life.

"They make a happy couple," people had said. "Young, intelligent yuppies, so much in love with life and each other!"

Romi and Jatin were engineers. Both were brilliant, keenly competitive and therefore always at loggerheads during their college days. Each vied with the other for the foremost rank. Studies were pursued with a one-track mind, hoping only to excel.

But there were fun moments too. The Engineering College functions were the talk of the town. If Jatin could dance, Romi could do it better. If Romi could sing, so could Jatin.

And so to the other college mates, the two were a pair of 'nuts', always plotting to outwit each other, fencing when they should be holding hands, at war when they should be making love, and ecstatic only when they were baiting each other.

But at the Graduation ceremony, the prospect of parting for good brought about an incredible transformation.

"Life will not be the same again when I've no one to compete with," Jatin said, "I feel lost already."

"I feel the same," mumbled Romi, "I'm going to miss you ever so much."

Her eyes were suddenly brimming over and Jatin diffidently offered her his handkerchief, hoping she wouldn't fling it back in his face. But she reached out for it and dabbed her eyes.

"Come now," Jatin said, tenderly putting his arms around her shoulder. "It's not the end of the world. May be we could meet sometime, have a meal together and get into a few arguments to keep us in form."

"But we're going to be miles apart, you in the east of India and I in the west."

"That's not such a great distance, unless of course, you'd like to move to the east near me."

"That wouldn't be a bad idea at all."

There were the usual rumblings in both homes. But this was just formality. Both belonged to rich and progressive families. Caste difference hardly mattered. The marriage too was a streamlined affair, with none of the pomp and pageantry of the wealthy.

Romi and Jatin made a fine pair. They were dedicated to their respective jobs, upwardly mobile but both feet planted firmly on the ground and anxious to make their presence felt in the changing world of engineering. Romi was also blessed with a good mother-in-law.

"Ma, I'm so glad I have you to run the place. I'm no good at housekeeping. I'd make a complete hash of it. I think I'm the luckiest girl in the world. A loving husband, a caring mother-in-law, and a well-run home – What more could anyone want in life!"

Mrs. Das was pleased. The girl was a rare combination of beauty and brains, culture and wealth.

Romi and Jatin had very few friends. They were not fond of socializing. An occasional bash was all they could squeeze into their hectic schedules. Then they would really let down their hair and freak out. But usually they preferred to take off by themselves to some remote hideout. Those were blissful moments.

As time went by, Mrs. Das began to feel a twinge of worry. Her friends threw veiled hints that the house had been empty for too long. The patter of little feet was long overdue.

"I've never interfered in their lives," she thought, "but perhaps they won't take too unkindly to some maternal advice."

That evening, she broached the subject. She felt awkward to intrude into something so private.

"Don't you both think it's time you started a family?" she asked timidly. "People are beginning to talk."

"To hell with people," Jatin answered, "It's none of their goddamned business."

"I'd like to have a baby," Romi said. "Perhaps we both need to see a doctor. We haven't been using contraceptives. But the baby just didn't materialize."

Jatin abruptly got up and moved away.

Later in bed, Romi asked, "What made you so irritable at the dinner table?"

She could feel him tense beside her.

"Because you made me feel that I'm to blame and that's not fair. You wanted to humiliate me in the presence of my mother."

"Come on. Stop imagining things. I never meant to accuse you. Obviously one of us is at fault. Or may be both. We're both good engineers, but we certainly don't know a lot about Biology. Perhaps we need to learn about our bodies."

Jatin was silent. He didn't reach out for her as he usually did.

"I'll go and see a gynecologist tomorrow," Romi said. "I'm not getting younger and the sooner we have a family, the better for the children. The job can always be put on hold."

"Yes, you do that," he mumbled, "But I'll be damned if I visit any doctor. You know quite well that I'm no impotent nincompoop. If I hadn't given you a good time in bed, you'd be the first to complain."

Romi had never seen her husband so upset before. He was overreacting. She had cast no aspersions on his fecundity. She had only stated facts.

"After all it takes two to make a baby," she thought, "and it needs to be conceived in love and not in anger."

The Gynaecologist had a string of degrees to her name. Romi had expected an elderly lady, but the woman behind the desk was perhaps her age. Romi stated her business briefly.

"You've come to the right place, Mrs. Das. This is the Infertility Clinic and we are here to help you. Let me first tell you that investigations for Infertility take a long time. We like to interview both partners together, rather than the woman only. And our investigations always begin with the male."

Romi looked worried. A small crease appeared on her forehead. The observant doctor placed her hand over Romi's. It felt warm and reassuring.

"I understand," she said, "your husband refuses to come. You're in good company. More than 50% of women coming to this clinic share your problem. The men think they are invulnerable."

Dr. Rekha took a thorough history of Romi. At the end of it she said, "The chances of either of you being infertile or subfertile is equal. But there is a negligible percentage, where infertility is unexplained. Let's start with your investigations."

She explained to Romi the things that needed to be done.

"Go ahead, Doctor, you run the whole gamut of tests. I'm not nervous."

Between Romi and Rekha, there was instant rapport. She gave the impression of being efficient and Romi felt confident.

At home, the cold war with Jatin continued. He showed no interest in Romi's account of her visit to the doctor. Also, his lackadaisical attitude in bed irritated her. What was once a joyful union now became a chore. Romi began wishing that night would never come. There were other changes too. They had always enjoyed each other's company, but now Jatin went out alone. Romi didn't complain.

One evening, she drove home early from office only to find that Jatin was already there. As she entered the porch, Jatin's voice carried through the window.

"I'm not to blame, Mother. The doctor says I'm a perfect specimen of health. It's Romi. Either she doesn't want to have a baby or she can't. Professional women are always selfish and self-centered. She couldn't be bothered with a child."

Romi had heard enough. She quietly got into her car, and drove away.

"I need to think. Why has Jatin turned against me? And why the lies?"

After a while, she pulled up at a café.

"I'll go in and have a cup of coffee," she thought. "I must compose myself before I go home."

She took the table near the window and looked out, her mind in turmoil. At first, she was not even conscious of a hand on her shoulder.

"Hey, a penny for your thoughts!" said Dr. Rekha. "Do you always go home so late?"

"Not usually. I felt like a cup of South Indian coffee," she said.

"May I join you?" Rekha asked. "I couldn't go home for lunch. And I still have a lot to do at the hospital. Thought I'd grab a bite before I fall to the floor."

The doctor sensed that all was not well with Romi.

"Are you worried about your tests? I've just been through the reports. Everything is fine. No structural deformities, hormones within normal limits, and you're ovulating. So you're bound to get pregnant sooner or later unless......"

"Unless what?"

"Unless the fault is with your husband. You better persuade him to have his tests done. There is no need to despair. Even those with low sperm counts can now be treated. I've got to rush now," Rekha said apologetically. "Drop in soon for your results. We can talk again."

Jatin was his normal self when she returned.

"How come you're late today?" he asked. "I was wondering what kept you."

"I had some work to finish. Did you get back early?"

"No, usual time," he bluffed.

That night, he took her in his arms as though nothing had happened.

"Have I imagined it all?" wondered Romi.

"I'd like you to meet some of my friends tomorrow. We are having an informal get-together," Jatin said.

Romi had half a mind to refuse, but seeing the imploring look on his face, she knew he was trying to make amends for a guilty conscience.

"Okay," she said, "It will be nice to go out for a change."

Romi knew many of the couples, but some were strangers. As they were all so friendly, she felt herself unwinding. Booze flowed freely and everyone seemed to be having a whale of a time. She stuck to her glass of sherry and refused a refill.

Jatin was quite merry with the whisky inside him. Dinner was a sumptuous affair. This was followed by a video show, which everyone seemed to be enjoying.

"Good Lord!" thought Romi, "Is this a blue film or am I being unusually prudish?"

The guy sitting next to her was becoming a nuisance. She could feel his hands creeping up her thigh. She wanted to signal Jatin that it was time to leave. But horror of horrors, she found that he had already slipped out.

"Relax Romi," the man was saying, "It's all in the game. Don't play the innocent with me. Jatin's gone off with my wife and it's only fair that I have you. Now don't say you've never heard of wife swapping parties? It happens all the time in high society. No strings attached. It just helps to take the monotony out of married life."

Romi had heard enough. The video was still on but the room was deserted except for the creep who kept pleading, "Come back, Romi. You've diddled me out of my fair share."

Romi went home and fell into bed, sobbing for most of the night. She must have fallen asleep towards morning. When she awoke, Jatin was standing there glaring at her in a rage.

"You stupid prude! You had to spoil the evening. What's so great about you anyway? You're just a barren hussy. You can't even start a family."

This was the last straw. She would have to teach Jatin a lesson.

"But wait, I'll bide my time. I'll make him eat his words," she thought.

Though she was fuming inside, Romi pretended that all was well between them. Jatin appeared contrite and blamed his behavior on the booze.

A few weeks later, Jatin phoned home from office. He was very busy with a project and would be working late.

"Romi, please do me a favor. I have left some diagrams in my drawer. I need them urgently. Could you send them over?"

She was rummaging through the files when she came across a doctor's bill. Why had Jatin been to a doctor when he had never been ill for a single day since their marriage?

Then it struck her. Perhaps he had gone for investigations too. The date showed that it was nearly a year old. Romi took down the name, address, and telephone number of the doctor. She didn't know what she would do. To barge in on the doctor and ask for details about her husband's investigations may not be the wise thing to do. He could claim the privilege of confidentiality in the doctor-patient relationship, or he could report the matter to Jatin. Perhaps Dr. Rekha could help. Romi decided to seek her advice.

"Yes, I know Dr. Rohit Duggal. We were classmates," Rekha said. "Perhaps he'll oblige, though it's been ages since we talked to each other. I can't promise anything but I'll try."

Dr. Duggal was pleased to hear Rekha's voice.

"What a pleasant surprise, young lady! It's wonderful to hear your voice again. But I know you aren't calling to inquire after my health. What can I do for you?"

"I have your patient Mr. Jatin Das sitting beside me," Rekha bluffed. "He has been tested for Infertility and was certified cent per cent normal by you. Could I have the reports of his tests?"

"Wait a minute. I'll have to look up the books. When did he say he came to me?"

Rekha gave him the month when the bill was issued.

It took only a few minutes for Dr. Duggal to give her the reports.

"What did you say Mr. Jatin told you? That the tests were within normal limits?" the doctor asked Rekha. "If it's the same guy who came to me, he's azoospermic. I advised him to have a testicular biopsy. But he never came back. You better send him back to me," said Dr. Duggal.

"Yes, I will. And thanks so much for the information. You've saved his wife unnecessary investigations."

"What did he say?" Romi asked anxiously.

"Your husband has no sperms at all."

"I can't believe it. He's healthy and certainly not lacking in libido."

"There is a difference between libido and infertility, Mrs. Das. Now there's only one way you can have a baby – artificial insemination by a donor."

Romi's face flushed with excitement. "That's exactly what I'll do. So go ahead, Doctor."

"But your husband will have to consent. He could create problems later like charging you with infidelity or sue me for impregnating you with sperm from a bank."

"How can he consent when he refuses to acknowledge that he is sterile? You've got to help me, Doctor," she pleaded.

"And lay my head on a chopping block?"

"Let me tell you something. Jatin is so desperate that he took me for a wife-swapping party and was happy to have me team up with his friend for the night. That is what made me suspicious. He thought he could fool the world if I did succeed in getting myself pregnant."

"Well, if that's the case, I'll stick my neck out for you."

A few months later, when Romi announced her blessed state to Jatin, he all but collapsed with surprise. But there was not much he could do. He had bragged about his potency to Romi and sworn to his mother that he was not at fault. There was no way he could back track now. He was a prisoner of his own lie.

"I thought you wanted a family very much," said Romi. "But now that I'm pregnant, you don't seem too happy about it."

"Of course I am, darling," he said, without a trace of enthusiasm. "I'm looking forward to becoming a father."

Romi knew that he was baffled.

"Could she have taken a lover," Jatin wondered. "How else could this have happened? How will I ever know? What a coward I am, not to come clean and take her into confidence!"

Plagued by doubts and suspicions, Jatin barely spoke to Romi. She knew pretty soon, a private investigator was trailing her. The guy was a novice and stuck out like a sore thumb. Romi smiled at his amateur attempts to hide whenever she looked directly at him. What made Jatin's life even more unbearable was the happiness of his mother. She just could not do enough for Romi. The tastiest dishes were painstakingly made for her. Mrs. Das fussed over her and attended to her every need.

Romi gave birth to a beautiful girl. Jatin kept up the semblance of a doting father. But inwardly, he was being consumed by doubts and fears. Romi bided her time for about three months. Then one day, she abruptly announced, "Jatin, I'm leaving you. I can't keep up the pretense that ours is an ideal family. Not for your sake or for your mother's. This way, we'll only end up hating each other. I need a break."

"But the child?" he asked.

"What of the child?" she challenged.

Jatin turned away before she could see him wince.

Mrs. Das couldn't stay away from her grandchild.

"None of this foolishness between you both can prevent me from enjoying her company," she said.

She insisted that the child be called Parinita, Pari for short. She brought back glowing reports of the child's milestones after each visit. Jatin listened silently. Inside was the terrible pain of rejection.

"But the fault is mine alone," he thought. "My stupid ego! If only I had unburdened myself to Romi!"

It took a whole year before Jatin could summon up the courage to call on Romi.

"I'm sorry. I wasn't honest with you. I guess it was my stinking pride. Or was it cowardice? I can't live without you. She will be ours."

"But you'll still have doubts. You'll still keep wondering who fathered the child. You'll start doubting every casual encounter of mine, with other men. Wouldn't that destroy even the memory of the good times we've had together?"

"No, I won't ask any questions. I want you home only on your conditions."

"I'm glad you've learnt your lesson, Jatin. I am just one of the many millions of women who suffer because of cowards like you. But I'm not stupid enough to send you away because I love you too. There is a time to be angry and a time to mend. Frankly, I don't know who the father is and

I'm not bothered about finding out. She was conceived with the help of a sperm bank, and it should make no difference to our relationship if we mean so much to each other."

RESURGENCE

Shirley was bubbling with joy. She had just received intimation from the office that she had bagged a seat for postgraduation in Paediatrics.

"It will mean three more years in the Medical College and Hospital. I'm glad I don't have to rush back home. I know Mum and Dad are anxious to see me settled. But I'm not ready to get married as yet."

Everyone loved Shirley. She came from Shillong and was a vivacious creature, always ready for fun and a little bit of harmless mischief. Anyone meeting her for the first time thought she was a saint. Her doe eyes and innocent smile camouflaged the real Shirley – the girl who played pranks on her classmates and had no qualms about pulling the legs of any lecturer she didn't like. Reggie her classmate, was the butt end of many of her practical jokes. He had endured it all through their years in Medical College because he had grown quite fond of her. And though she felt the same about Reggie, no one could get her to admit that she had a soft corner for him.

"I wonder if Reggie will be pleased that I'll be around for another three years to pester him," she thought, "I hear that he too has been selected for a PG course in Surgery."

But her joy was short-lived. Her father had been diagnosed with Bone Cancer and had to undergo an amputation of his left leg, followed by a long period of intermittent chemotherapy.

"Come home Darling," her mother begged, "I won't be able to take care of him on my own. You can surely put your PG course on hold."

Shirley had no option but to go home. It broke her heart to leave the college which she so loved, and Reggie who had become an important part of her life.

"What can be more important than the welfare of my Dad? I just have to go home."

She soon realised that more was expected of her.

"You know I won't live very long," he said, "I can die in peace if you are married into a good family, with a husband to take care of you."

Shirley watched all her ambitions go up in smoke.

"I believed that I could have my own clinic after postgraduation and take care of those many sick tribal children in this area. Their parents can't take them to hospitals far away nor can they afford to go to expensive private practitioners."

"You can still do it after marriage. No husband in this day and age will prohibit his doctor wife from working," said her mother confidently.

The man who presented himself as her prospective groom took her breath away. All thoughts of postgraduation or of Reggie evaporated. Martin was like an Adonis, tall, well built, broad shouldered, with a smile that made her body tingle all over. His dark eyes held hers with the promise of a great future. Martin was an IPS officer of the rank of Police Inspector. Shirley admired the quiet dignity with which he conducted himself both in speech and manners.

"I'm sure we'll be happy together," she thought, "I wish we could know each other better before we tie the knot."

But there was not much time for courting. Her father was sinking rapidly and he insisted that the marriage be speeded up.

"I have only one request to make," he told Martin, "Don't take her away immediately. Let her stay till I breathe my last."

He would never know the frustrations that marriage brought to Shirley.

Though Martin loved Shirley to distraction, she could never understand his possessiveness. For a sprightly young woman who loved her freedom, she felt manacled by his love. Did men not want successful wives? Did they only want subordinate women for long-term relationships?

"I'm a full-fledged doctor. Why don't you let me take up a job?"

"I'm earning enough for both of us. There is no need for you to work."

"It's not the wage that I'm after. I could do honorary work in a hospital or clinic. So many children are suffering from health problems. I could be of help."

"You are my wife and I am your first priority. Learn to be a good wife and that's all I ask. Consider yourself the queen of my domain."

"Then you believe that successful women cannot be good housewives?"

He was stubborn and unreasonable on this particular subject. It led to many tiffs between them.

"Do you want to keep me dependent and subjugated always?"

"You have freedom to do whatever you want at home. You can form your own circle of friends and take part in all kinds of activities. But I won't share you with your profession. I know it will take up all your time. I want a full-time wife."

Martin was often away from home for several days at a time. Shirley was lonely. Her frustrations added to her boredom and irritability. There was only so much time she could spend on reading or listening to music or watching TV.

"I must do something before I go into depression. There must be ways to snap out of this emotional isolation," she thought, "There are many women who are happy and content in their roles of stay-at-home wives. I need not feel unfulfilled or inferior in any way. I will turn my attention to culinary skills and become a good cook."

"That's a very good idea Darling," said her mother, "I'll give you all my best recipes. Try to excel in whatever you do. Perhaps Martin is not as confident as he appears to be. He may be suffering from some inferiority complex. In a few years he may change and even let you take up a job."

"It may be too late. I may have forgotten all about Medicine by then," Shirley moaned.

"You need to introspect. Do you love Martin enough to want to see him happy? Then you must be willing to let go of your own preferences. In marriage, one or the other will have to adjust. If you truly love him, then your personal ambitions and aspirations will have to take a back seat. Compromise is not weakness. It shows strength of character."

Shirley took her mother's advice seriously. She put her heart and soul into cooking. Martin noticed a change in her behaviour. She reverted to her old chirpy self as she used to be in the early months of their marriage. She kept humming to herself as she went about her chores.

"Something has changed," Martin thought, "Why, even the dishes she puts on the table are tastier these days."

"Hey Shirley!" he said, "Your cooking seems to have improved a lot. At this rate I'm sure to develop a paunch."

"If I can't be a doctor, I can at least be a good cook," she laughed. "I'm glad you noticed the change in my cooking.

I've invested in a new cook book and I keep pestering my friends for new recipes." He gave her a hug. "I'm so glad you don't resent me for keeping you away from your profession."

Shirley realised that happiness comes from choosing one's attitude in any given circumstance. Now she had her own cookery website. Through her blogs she gave advice on Food and Nutrition, Blending of Spices, Budgeting of food income, Art of Serving and other matters useful to housewives. In addition, there were easy recipes which any novice could try her hand at. Martin was totally oblivious of her popularity on the Net. Visitors to her site were in thousands. Many wrote to her for advice. She patiently answered each of their queries.

Then one day, she saw an announcement of a cookery contest to be held by Master Chefs of Australia. The best, uncomplicated, easy recipe for small income groups would receive $5000/- and a trip to Australia for the annual Food Festival in Melbourne.

"Nothing like trying," Shirley thought, "I believe I can succeed if I put my mind to it."

Shirley quizzed her maid about the easy recipes she cooked for her family.

"Madam, rather than tell you, why don't you come to my house and I'll cook a meal for you? Of course, that is if you don't consider it below your dignity to eat at my house. I know you've got your prestige to keep as a police officer's wife."

"Let me think. Sahib will be out of station for two days next week. Can I come on one of those days? No one need know about it."

The simplicity of the meal impressed Shirley. The Junglee Pulao that the maid had prepared was rice cooked with a variety of greens and herbs grown in her garden. There was a side dish made out of pumpkin flowers and stems and a chutney of onion, red chillies and tamarind mixed with a teaspoon of coconut oil.

"I've never tasted such a meal before," she told her maid. "Now I know how you keep so healthy. You're quite an innovator."

"We have to make do with what grows in our little vegetable patch Madam. I have two growing children to feed and a husband who is ravenous after a day's work."

Shirley wrote out the recipe and sent it off with not much hope of receiving a prize. A month later, a phone call from the Master Chef himself told her that she had won the prize for the cheap simple recipe. He had prepared and tasted the food himself and found it both nutritious and delicious. Of course he had to hunt through the Indian shops in Melbourne to find suitable greens and herbs.

Now Shirley had to break the news to Martin. She wondered how he would react. But she was in for a surprise.

"Congrats Darling!" he said, "From doctor to chef! What an enterprising wife! Am I proud of you!"

He drew her into his arms and gave her a hug.

"How did you know?" she asked.

"I've known for a long time. My colleague's wife is one of your ardent fans. He brought me the good news this morning. He said the prize was announced on the Master Chef's Face Book."

Shirley was truly happy. Though she had sacrificed her profession as a doctor, she had clung to her marriage for better or for worse. This was Shirley's Resurgence.

www.ingramcontent.com/pod-product-compliance
Lightning Source LLC
LaVergne TN
LVHW091312150826
845673LV00006B/1623

* 9 7 9 8 8 8 8 1 5 6 4 4 5 *